A GENTLEMAN WOULD
NOT LIKE IT

A GENTLEMAN WOULD NOT LIKE IT

Angela Myers

The Book Guild Ltd
Sussex, England

First published in Great Britain in 2004 by
The Book Guild Ltd
25 High Street
Lewes, East Sussex
BN7 2LU

Typesetting in Times by
SetSystems Ltd, Saffron Walden, Essex

Printed in Great Britain by
CPI Bath

A catalogue record for this book is
available from the British Library

ISBN 1 85776 881 7

To Will Vaughan, in whose very enjoyable tutorials I first encountered Dr Monro.

1794

Thomas's diary

This Thursday morning it came to me. The night before, just as we were preparing for bed, Hannah suddenly said, 'There's not much you can do for them in Bethlem, really, is there?' It was my own fault; I'd been describing some of the conditions I found there last Wednesday on my visit as Head Physician. I was complaining because some of the improvements which I suggested, I know the governors will never make however much I complain; so of course it was silly of me to go on to defend the place from her criticism. But of course I said there *were* things we could do and that some lunatics did recover and get discharged from the hospital, cured.

May the Lord God never send any of my family mad, is all I ever ask. But her question set me thinking. If I'm not doing any good as a doctor – and of course I would debate that one, after all there is my private practice too – then what *can* I do?

Then that morning I was looking out over the river, first the muddy banks of low tide, and then the sparkling water in the winter sun, then the Shot Tower opposite which many a time I've tried to sketch, picking up my porte-crayon and wishing I was outdoors and it was summer again.

At that moment the thought entered my head of those sketches I'd seen at my barber's in Maiden Lane the other day, done by his son, he told me. Very proud he was. I took a second look and it wasn't just him talking, though he does

1

that all right. They were extraordinarily good for a lad of 18 or whatever he is, and I actually bought one.

It wasn't very expensive, of course, though plenty for a barber's son, and I thought when I got it home and put it up on the wall it would shrink in significance, but it did not; instead it seemed to glow there on my study wall. A marshy foreground, hills and a sun which really seemed to light up.

And then it came, as I said, while I looked at that Shot Tower and smarting a little from Hannah's remark, 'There's not much you can do for them, is there?'

'Maybe not much,' I said to myself, and I think my lips actually moved. But I *can* help that lad, and myself at the same time, if I ask him to come and draw for me, either views out of the window or maybe copying some of the pictures I've got already.

Hannah would smile. She thinks I've got far too many watercolours which clutter up the place. I could pay him a little or maybe give him a good meal for his pains. His parents aren't that well off and they say the mother's difficult, not to say a little off her head. The father would be gratified; I would at least ensure a good haircut for myself for the rest of my life!

As to the boy himself, he seemed a bit surly when I bought the sketch, but we'd see if his tone changed at a chance of mixing with gentlemen and maybe selling his pictures. And not just for the few shillings that I'd pay him for the evening's work. But I leap ahead of myself.

I sat down there and then and started to envisage it. I could have him in here by the window, if I moved the furniture round a bit. Hannah might not like it; she might think him a bit scruffy to have in the house. Well, she *would* think so; no doubt about it. But then she's got the babies upstairs. I'm not needed at the moment, except as a provider of course.

Three boys, who would have thought it? Tom, after me,

she says, though he is really Edward Thomas; Henry, only three and already wanting to sit and draw beside me if he isn't yelling; and the baby, Robert. And she's in the family way again.

She says she is sure it's a girl this time. Poor thing, a house full of men later on wouldn't be easy for her. But, thank goodness I could afford this new house where the nursery is a nice long way from the drawing room!

I knew we had to get out of Bedford Square when the third child was on its way and what with my new salary at Bethlem, the private madhouses I now run after Father died, and the sale of some of Father's collection, we had enough and Hannah is pleased to be so grand.

We have illustrious neighbours here: Garrick's widow, no less, and Henderson, the art collector. We two are fast becoming friends. It is a marvellous new building, this Adelphi; right on the river, though Hannah worried that it would smell from being on the waterside; and central too, both for the gentry one side of us and the artists' quarter on the other. I *am* proud to be a father I suppose but I'm prouder still to be a Fellow of the Royal College of Physicians and of owning some excellent works of art, not just the few I kept from my father's sale when he died, but those I have managed to add, of my own taste.

I started to wonder whether I would show that boy of Turner's my collection. I looked at the walls and started to dream about acquiring some Gainsboroughs. I met him once and in a small way he is my hero, his having been so kind to me as a lad and his style just what I would like to emulate. But I was dreaming again. I sprang up. 'No time like the present,' and I set out for Maiden Lane without debating with myself further as to the suitability of what I was doing.

He might be interested, I thought as I walked along, in the one or two sketches I've lately been given by Cozens, the madman I took on this last February. I'm not sure I'd have done it if people like Beaumont, with all his wealth and love of art, and Farington, who is now a member of the new Royal Academy, hadn't said they'd get up a fund to help pay for him. They didn't want to see him in the filth of Bedlam, as they so tactfully put it.

Of course I didn't know him before he went mad; he's been to Italy with Payne Knight and again with Beckford (poor fellow, no wonder he cracked!). They pay a guinea a week for him and I've set Holmes to care for him. Holmes is a safe hand. I pop over to Hackney to see him in Brooke House once a week, on my regular visit there. He talks and laughs nineteen to the dozen. Indeed I cannot communicate with him, because he never lets anyone interrupt him.

So I don't see much hope of a recovery for poor John Cozens, but the sketches are excellent. He seems to favour the darkness of shadow and caves a good deal. That's what Beaumont picked out. I thought, however, there were some quite open sunny ones too. I liked his technique, but I haven't had that much time lately to study quite how he achieves it. This morning was the first one of leisure I have enjoyed for many a week.

When I reached the barber's shop I was less able to know where to begin than I had thought. Mr Turner came forward to greet me but looked a little puzzled, seeing as I had only just had my hair cut the other day. I could see from the press in the shop that we would find it hard to be alone, so I asked if I could sit down awhile and look at some of his son's work in the cellar, where he exhibits the pictures.

He was all smiles then and I sat alone for a few minutes before he managed to excuse himself to come downstairs. He lifted himself up and down on his toes in a way I've noticed he does when he is enthusiastic; he is a small man and needs the height, I suppose. I imagine he thought I had come back to buy another picture.

4

I coughed and said something like, 'I was wondering whether I could do your lad a good turn.' He looked pleased, but when I suggested the boy could work at my house once a week copying pictures in return for a meal and a small remuneration, he only asked, 'How much?' I was expecting a little more surprise and delight, I must say.

I suggested 2s 6d, which he considered for a few minutes, looking very dubious. Then he asked me whom I knew in the art world, which I considered a presumption. But then I recalled that it is not always easy to do favours for people, being as they are quite often ungrateful. However, the names Hearne and Beaumont and my having once sketched with Gainsborough must surely have impressed him.

The upshot was he went to get his son.

I was very interested to see what sort of lad this was on better acquaintance.

This time he was more polite, obviously having been primed by his father. His nose seems to dominate his face like his father's, he is equally small of stature and looks energetic. He spoke with a strong accent as his father does, but somewhat different in region I fancied, and listened gravely to my proposition. He did not, however, beam with gratitude as I had dreamt he would. Instead he reminded me he had already won a Silver Palette at the Royal Academy where he went some evenings to draw.

His father interrupted. 'Will goes about each summer sketching in the countryside; he's already been to Wales, Oxford, Canterbury, Bristol.'

'And what sort of studies do you prefer doing?' I asked, turning to the boy, looking down at him.

'I like to study buildings,' he said, 'especially abbeys and castles when I can find them. Topographical views are easier to sell than most.'

'One of my close friends is Hearne,' I said, unaware that

5

I now seemed to be courting him rather than he, me. 'I expect you know his volumes of topographical subjects?'

The lad nodded.

There was a silence. So I said, 'Shall I expect you, say on Friday evenings for a few hours, starting tomorrow? I live on the river in the new Adelphi buildings. Number 8.' I thought that would impress. Everyone, perhaps barring the Turners, had been talking of Adam's new project and I was lucky to have been able to buy one of the houses in the terrace soon after it was finished.

There was no answer. But the father seemed to be hinting something when he said, 'The good doctor is the principal physician at Bethlem Hospital. He also has a private mental home in Hackney. And has lately taken on the cure of the artist Cozens.' I remembered I had told him that when he was cutting my hair last week.

At this the boy brightened and suddenly shot out his hand and shook mine, agreeing to come the next night.

I started to walk back home, feeling suddenly very hungry, so that I hoped that the incident of a servant leaving this morning had not caused bad temper in our cook, which might spoil the dinner I was about to eat.

But then I heard footsteps behind me; I turned and the boy Will Turner was there. 'Sir,' he panted, 'I know another lad my age who would like to come with me; his name is Tom Girtin.'

'Well,' I said, 'I don't just take on any *Tom*, Dick or Harry to paint at my house. Who is this Girtin?'

'He works with me at Smith's, sir, the engraver. We colour in prints for him. He has no end of talent, but he doesn't have the luck I have to show off his pictures at his father's house.' I said nothing for a moment, wondering whether the lad, however cocksure in some ways, was a little afraid to enter a gentleman's house on his own. Would I lose him if I said no to his friend?

6

'Tell me,' I said finally, 'have you been given lessons, apart from at the Academy? How did you begin?'

'Oh, I worked in a dirty dark hole with a man of the name of Lowe. He calls himself a history painter, but it's full of brats, sir, you can't get nothing done and he drinks. Otherwise I get practice, as I said, sir, painting outdoors in the style of Wilson, and I work for Smith sometimes. Malton I'm very obliged to too, sir, I got a bit of learning with him, 'cos my father came into a little money from a grateful customer and he was persuaded by a gentleman to spend it on articling me to Malton; he's an architectural draughtsman and lives close by here.'

To say I was surprised is a vast understatement. I hadn't heard of all this teaching and travels. I thought I was about to help an unknown lad, though I was a fool to think no one else but me would have noticed his talent, as he is not exactly a child. I said, a little abruptly, because he now seemed to *want* to talk, out of the range of his father's ears perhaps, 'Yes, bring Girtin along and we'll see how he shapes.'

'Thank you, sir,' he said, and ran off.

Hannah, as I predicted, was not impressed. I told her while we were at dinner.

'Two common lads, eating under our roof. Have you gone mad, Thomas? What about our little lads?'

'They won't even see them and I don't think I've gone mad,' I said. 'I hope it isn't catching.' My wry little joke made her smile at least.

'But what is the point, Thomas?'

And then I told her it had been her comment about my not being able to help the Bethlem patients which had sparked it off. She blushed, and her eye which has the squint looked worse for a minute.

'Is it because you are an artist yourself? Do you want to learn from them?' she asked, pleating the white tablecloth

7

between her fingers. 'But surely you must know more than they do. They're only young.' I was just about to answer when she continued, 'What do you want the copies for? Or do you merely want to help poor lads? Because there are plenty of charities which we could give to without having the house full of smelly boys.'

'They may not be polished but they aren't smelly, or at least the Turner lad isn't. I haven't met Tom Girtin as yet. Yes, I think I would like to imagine myself the sort of man who helps struggling artists, but I also want to add to my collection and I flatter myself, my dear, that I know talent when I see it.'

'Oh, your collection!' she said, laughing. 'We'll have to move again soon or it'll start flowing out of the doors and windows!' I was silent. 'But you haven't even seen Girtin's pictures?' she added, daintily wiping her mouth, disappointed I didn't laugh at her joke.

'No, but if I don't like them I shall send him away. Perhaps it is asking too much to hope he is as good as Will Turner appears to be. You know, he's already won a Silver Palette at the new Academy; his father says quite a few people have bought his pictures too. It isn't just me. I think I was quite lucky to get him to come when I asked. I fancy he was taken with the name Cozens.'

'Cozens?' she said, puzzled.

'An artist patient I took on at Brooke House at the request of Beaumont. He has gone mad quite suddenly. It was in February. I think I did mention it to you.'

'Should I have heard of him?' she said, wiping her mouth and signalling to the new servant to take the dishes away.

'He has been on the Grand Tour with two famous collectors, but I privately think he has no chance of returning to his right mind. I've seen this sort of mania before. Yes, I will have some of that cheese, thank you.'

In a little while, after she had refused the cheese and sat

8

thinking, she said, 'I know you, Thomas, you'll soon tire of this philanthropy. In any case you've got too much on your plate already. You were only the other night talking of renting a country house for the summers, so that has to be found and furnished if you're serious. Then there's all your travelling to see patients, Bethlem Hospital work, your own sketching, let alone your family. They come a poor last as usual!'

'Oh my dear,' I said, finishing my wine and preparing to rise from the table, 'It is I who feel an outcast with all these babies who have come so rapidly to join us.'

She blushed and squinted again. 'I know what a proud father you are, Thomas. You would not wish us back into the childless state surely.'

'No, seeing how it becomes you so much to be a mother,' I said, and she left me, all smiles again.

The next evening I sat waiting for the two lads to come. Six o'clock came and went and I began to fidget. The Shot Tower was clear and beautiful across the river in the moonlight. I fingered the prints that Henderson next door had lent me, which had been done with the help of the camera lucida. They were of shipping around Dover. I had decided to start the boys on the task of copying these, and see how they shaped up.

At seven minutes past the servant showed them in. Turner's companion was a very dark swarthy lad with a large nose, just as Turner and I have – though mine I like to think is more distinguished – rather full lips and close-cropped hair which made him look almost like a French revolutionary. Hannah would certainly not like this, and I was glad she had decided to keep right away from the downstairs rooms while the boys were there. She was, she told me, to be found if wanted, taking tea in the drawing room.

I showed them their two desks which I had put end to

end so that they could share the same water pot. They looked about them, Girtin a little furtively, Turner with more obvious interest. He went to the window. 'Can we start by painting the water, sir? I'd really like to be able to paint the way the lights move on it.'

'Not yet,' I said, 'Maybe later, another day.'

'I like the river, sir, and the ships. I was at Brentford for a year when I were ten and I painted a lot of river scenes then. And I was at Margate.'

I merely nodded and he subsided. He has a surprisingly deep voice for a small lad.

I showed them a few of my collected Rookers and Dayes and Salvator Rosas. While we were looking, Girtin let drop that he had worked for Dayes.

'And how did you get on with the master?' I said.

'Not well,' he said. 'I ended up in Tothill Fields.' He gave a short laugh before seeing my face.

Oh dear, I thought to myself, shall I encourage him to tell me the circumstances of his imprisonment or should I go and speak to Dayes himself? I decided I would see Dayes. I knew him a little and had bought some of his work. I can't say I had taken to him personally, whereas there was something likeable about Tom Girtin.

I quickly showed them to their seats and told them to copy the pictures that Henderson had lent me. If Girtin was no good I would terminate his employment straight away.

'Am I to colour his work, sir?' Turner asked, indicating Girtin.

'Well, yes, if you wish to start like that.'

'Only you see, sir, Tom is better at the outlines, that's what Smith always says.'

Tom Girtin glowered a little but they sat down and began. They had a candle between them which I thought adequate, as the fire burnt up brightly enough to give more light as well as warmth, for it was a cold night.

10

After a while I went upstairs to Hannah, who gave me some tea from her new silver teapot which she prizes so highly, but I came downstairs again towards the end of the four hours. They were flagging a little in their efforts and were glad to see the servant entering behind me with two bowls of oysters, which I had decided not to stint on, and two hunks of bread.

It was not a pleasant sight to watch either of them eat, especially Will Turner who had no table manners and kept wiping his mouth on his sleeve and licking the juice off the shells. I thought Tom Girtin was trying harder to impress, perhaps because he knew he was on probation.

After the first minute or so, I went over and had a good look at what they had turned out, an occupation preferable to watching the progress of the food into their mouths. Girtin indeed was a wonderful draughtsman, and Turner's colour sense was subtle and unexpected. I had put the money down beside their plates and they pocketed the coins cheerfully, without saying so much as thank you.

Then Turner began to question me and I was not surprised to find he wanted to know more about Cozens.

I promised I would show him what sketches I had of his when the oysters were finished. I feared they might spatter the pictures if I let them near them as they ate. A servant came in with a bowl and a towel and the boys looked a little confused at first but when I indicated they should wash their hands, they did so. Then I went to a desk and got out the Cozens studies. They studied the sketches carefully, commenting on them together. Turner, like Beaumont, was interested in the dark cave and ravines he had done.

'Do you, too, wish to travel to Italy and the Alps?' I asked them.

'Yes,' Turner said without hesitation. 'Like Wilson. His grandeur in Welsh mountain scenes comes from studying the Alps.'

11

'Oh yes,' I said dryly. 'Well, I think we have plenty of grandeur in our own country not to worry about studying mountains in Italy.'

Who did this lad think he was, telling me about grandeur in art?

Girtin seemed to agree with me. 'I like studying buildings better than mountains,' he said.

'And would you like to attend the Academy schools with Turner here?'

'I reckon so.' But the somewhat surly admission was belied by the lively expression on his face a second later.

As soon as I had put the pictures away, I asked the new servant to see them out, saying I would expect them next Friday at six o'clock.

The servant came back. 'I'm afraid one of the lads spat in the hallway, sir, shall I clean it up?' The word 'spat' came out with all the disdain he could muster.

'Oh yes, please, Stevens,' I said. 'Was it the smaller of the two?'

'Yes sir.'

Should I keep Turner on if he was going to sully the new house like this, and should I keep Girtin, the ex-prisoner and possible revolutionary?

Even though I feared what Hannah would say, I already knew I would keep them both.

*

Girtin hurried to keep up with Turner as they walked into the mistiness of the river's edge.

'You shouldn't have told him I did the outlines. Now I'll get stuck with them.'

'*If* he keeps you on. He'll check with Dayes and *he* won't give you much of a recommendation.'

'Dayes is insane, he should be in one of Monro's madhouses!' He laughed. 'Grand house, I'm sure he expected us both to ooh and ah when he showed us in . . . and he had some good stuff on his walls. I think I spotted a Canaletto. I shall ask him next time if I dare. What's the point of his getting us copying, do you think?'

Turner wriggled from under the hand Tom Girtin had put on his shoulder. 'Probably thinks he'll sell them when we're famous,' he grinned. 'He's an artist himself, my dad says.'

'Oh?'

'Well, he sketches when he's out on his horse travelling to see the mad people.'

'Perhaps it soothes him. They do say Bethlem is full of stench and chains and people screaming and groaning.'

'Most probably, but we'll never know; they don't let visitors in now like they used to. No one knows what goes on; they probably "disappear" if they get too awkward. In any case, he's got at least one private madhouse as well; I don't suppose he spends too much time at Bedlam!'

'Will you come back next Friday?' Girtin asked.

'Oh yes. My dad says Monro's got good contacts and he's not a bad old fellow. At least the oysters were good and there was plenty of bread.'

'The fire was kept roaring hot, too, though one candle seemed stingy to me. I shall ask for another one.'

'Dare you to! He'll say no. You can see it in his face; that beaky nose and his beetling brows! Did you notice the way he looked down his long nose at us?'

Tom laughed. 'Is he married, with brats?'

'Yes, but he wouldn't call them so; my dad says he's got two or three, little ones. I don't suppose we'll see them. They won't bother us; I like children but not when I'm working. He's got plenty of rooms in that place. What would I give to have a house on the river like that. Wish he

13

would set us to draw out of his window instead of copying those boats that Henderson did, not to mention the Cozens tracings of Lake Como and Monte Casino!'

'Better than things Dayes set me to do, or Smith for that matter. Remember that *Moralist* he did a few years ago? That one with the prostitutes and the old man "lecturing" them? He certainly has it both ways with those sorts of pictures. Do you remember how one of the customers sniggered?' Both lads laughed at the recollection. 'Hey Will, I've never met anyone like that before. Smith's lot he mixes with are bohemian all right, but this is elegance and fine living. Him being a doctor, I wonder if he could cure me when I get one of my attacks when I can't breathe properly.'

'He cures the mad, not the sick. This is where I turn off. See you, Tom.'

1795

Thomas's diary

It's exactly a year since I first took on Turner and Girtin. Since then another child's been born. To think I am a father of four. Sally, we call her. I was a little loath to choose that name, as Sarah, Hannah's sister, was not very respectable, but I said as long as it was Sally I didn't mind. Perhaps Hannah misses her sister, though she never speaks of her without sniffing.

She was right about it being a girl, and how pleased she was. I too. I hear myself predicting all sorts of talents for them, as fond parents will. If one scribbles I think he is an artistic genius, if another beats time to a tune, however imperfectly, I imagine he will be another Handel! Well it is early days, but I hope they all will enjoy the pleasures of drawing and painting as I do! Maybe now we shall see an end to childbearing. Hannah has not been so hearty since Sally's birth and she herself feels that her quiver is full enough.

My patronising of Tom and Will, as I know them now, has continued this winter. I was glad I did not believe the evil rumours that Dayes put about concerning Tom. He is still furious that Tom broke his apprenticeship agreement and survived Tothill Fields. The general opinion in the art world is that he was jealous of the boy. Dayes called Tom dissolute but I see no sign of it. Perhaps he means he womanises, or does he associate him with the French because of his hair? But that is nothing to me so long as it

15

doesn't come between him and his work. Tom is quite charming and often quite witty in his manner, I find, once he got over his first shyness. Will will never be anything but crude and, in his quiet way, pleased with himself. Also I fear he is sly in the way he often blames Tom for the spilling of a water bottle or a blot on the paper. Tom for his part denies it, but does not insist if Will continues to exonerate himself at his expense. Tom probably realises that I have understood Will's character and knows I will not blame him for something that Will has so obviously done.

They both have extraordinary talent in my opinion, and I never cease to pat myself on the back that I took the step I did last year. Hannah continues to stay upstairs during their visits when she can, but she is more curious and more involved than she pretends. Of course there was an outcry that Tom was a pro-French activist with that haircut, and a horror that Will might come near our babes and infect them with his coarse language and manner. She is not really very interested in their genius; she probably thinks I exaggerate it. She has always tended to humour me over my love of watercolours and, as the babies increase in number, is less and less interested in what sincerely moves and motivates me, if I am honest with myself. However, she is a good and diligent wife and mother so I must not complain, not even when she refuses to come out in the evening with me, as she often does now, because her squint worsens. I tell her it does not, but it is true that she has a strange cast to her face these days which when I courted her was hardly noticeable, or if it was, it added to her charm. It is lucky she is content to be a mother and leaves me to my own interests and friends, though occasionally I would love her to be at my side when instead she is probably at home singing a lullaby to her infants.

We now are the proud owners, or rather we *rent*, a fine property in Surrey in the village of Fetcham near Dorking.

The house was built in 1791, so it is pretty new. I am most happy with the idea of using it in the summer months. It is better for the children to be away from the smells of London which grow worse in the heat, and it's so noisy too. Another advantage is that I am now able to ask the lads over to sketch from nature there. Tom has been rarely but Will is an energetic walker who thinks nothing of distances. In that way he reminds me of myself before I got this infernal limp.

I told him once that I got it when I fell heavily, playing tennis with the Prince, but he was not to be impressed. He probably did not believe me. Maybe the Prince does not mean much to him. He is more interested in the rich and noble who buy art. I have not heard that the Prince is interested in art. Women and clothes are more in his line. Will Turner has recently sold pictures to Hoare of Stourhead and to that millionaire idiot Beckford himself. It has been a fast journey indeed from the days when his father sold his pictures for between one and three shillings.

I told him I would not be seen dead with Beckford in my house, who I said looks more like a picture dealer than a gentleman collector and one of the richest men in England; but both lads have benefited from meeting my friends Hearne and Hoppner at Adelphi Terrace. Hoppner has great influence in the Royal Academy and Hearne's volumes of British landscapes are second to none. I know that they have been round to Henderson's and have copied some of his Maltons, or at least Tom showed me something he did there for him. I do not feel any fear of letting them join the conversaziones on other evenings of the week, for I know their so-called copies will be a passport into any artist's group. Laporte, from whom I once took lessons myself, they have also met. I am less keen on his work than I was, I have to say.

Hearne was interested in what they had done, especially

copies of his own work which he had lent me. We laughed over several copies that Will had made of a mill by my friend. I had insisted that Will copy it several times until it was to my satisfaction. I saw a stubborn look come over his face but he did it. He likes to colour much more than to draw, of course, and he is really extraordinarily subtle in his shading. Girtin draws like an angel but has asked several times if he can colour and I have so far said no. He sulks for a while and then luckily recovers.

He seems much interested in drawings I have by Canaletto. He showed me another sketch he did in the old ruins of the Savoy Palace, which anyone could see was indebted to the Italian.

I have for my sins listened into some of their conversations when they are copying. I gather that Tom spends all his money but that Will saves his. Tom, it seems, is generous and a bit overgenerous too; whereas Will, like his father, is canny and never lends or gives anything away.

Will is not averse to telling me what the newspapers have to say about work which he has shown at the Academy. The *St James Chronicle*, for instance, said his pictures were well chosen and well coloured. He has told me that on more than one occasion. And the *Morning Post*, that he had an eye for nature and he should not look to any other source than this. This was one of the reasons I suggested they come out to Fetcham, though Hannah is not really satisfied with the state of the place as yet. Tom Girtin has shown at the Academy, his *Ely Cathedral*, but I don't think it was noticed among all the others in the Antique Academy. All these watercolours have to be glazed and I found it hard not to get a glare on the glass from the windows, when I went to see them.

Turner always tells Girtin to travel and sketch from life, so that his ruins have more character and are not just copies of Canaletto's or Moore's work; then it turned out Girtin

18

had been on a recent tour with Moore to draw Lichfield and Lincoln Cathedrals. Even so Will Turner stresses he must go on his own, so he is not told which facade to paint or how to paint it. That is partly why I hope he will come to Surrey, where I should not attempt to influence him in choice of subject matter; but I think he is keener to sketch something more ruinous and sublime, like Tintern Abbey or the big castles of the north.

Hannah made a huge fuss about moving to the new house last April and then another fuss when we came back in October. It is an undertaking, but she does not have to arrange it, only to suffer it, and in the carriage with two nursemaids I don't think her lot can be said to be that hard.

'It is I, my dear,' I told her, 'who should fuss. I have much further to go to see to my Bethlem patients twice a week from Fetcham and to see my private patients too.' Thank God for a good horse and a healthy physique when I am on the road much of the time. I also take with me a sketching kit and often extend my hour's picnic by a little extra so that I may record the spot I sit in. Then in the evening I transfer the sketch, using wet paper and Indian ink. I flatter myself I get better at water effects and I think my trees and bushes have improved, perhaps with the influence of Cozens. That is what Tom suggested when he observed me the other day. Sometimes I wonder who is the master here and who are the pupils! They certainly do not take kindly this year to being taught by me, and I try to hold my tongue when I see something that can be easily rectified in what they do.

I have had a netting put inside the roof of my carriage now, a thing I have been meaning to do for a long time. I can put any particular favourites from my portfolio in it and while away a tedious journey by studying them. That is, on a longer journey, when I am not on horseback. If it is wet or snowy I prefer a carriage to a horse!

Farington saw what I had done and teased me, saying I was copying Beaumont who apparently has the same thing in his carriage, where he carries his Claude of *Hagar and the angel* to gloat over while travelling. I could honestly retort that I had no idea Sir George had such a device and that I never copied anyone in my life.

That put Farington out of countenance.

Will was pleased to meet my new Fetcham neighbour, Locke of Norbury Hall, whom I waited on very early in my stay in April or May. He is a banker, an agreeable man and a true art lover. I think he disliked Will when they met, but he changed his attitude when he saw his work. It is a pity Tom does not try as hard as Will to get patrons. On the face of it one would think he would have much more chance of pleasing a patron, being a more agreeable personality generally. I think that Locke's friend Angerstein, very rich and a great collector, may buy from Will too, should he play his cards right.

I am always surprised that with this money that William is accruing, he does not disdain my humble 3s 6d this winter. Tom, I think, is more in need of it still. I know from overhearing them chatting over their work that Will has taken rooms adjoining his parents' place in Maiden Lane, rather than staying at home with them. I am not entirely surprised; his mother is an angry and violent woman from what I have heard. His father finds her difficult and has more than once been hit by a chair or pot thrown at him. Maybe this is true of Will also. I know, from listening in to the lads, that Will very often spends evenings with Mr Wills, another art lover who has a house in Sevenoaks and one in Mount Street. I heard him tell Tom how much he enjoyed playing with the children there. That was a surprise. He never struck me as a kindly or fun-loving lad. I suspect he walks all the way to Sevenoaks; no distance seems to deter him.

20

I admire a good walker, I used to be one myself but this limp is a drawback.

Poor Tom, I wonder if he will live to have children. He has had several attacks of breathlessness here which frighten him. I can see it in his eyes. He is pathetically grateful for anything I do to relieve the symptoms, but he told me once he thinks he will not live to become famous. I did my best to reassure him, but I do not want him to be too sure of his genius or to take on the superior airs and graces of Will, whom at times I find a trial.

Farington, who came to visit us in Fetcham, has said he will try to use his influence with the Academy to get Tom into the Schools there; but I fear that Dayes's version of the past coupled with Tom's revolutionary appearance may put people off. Farington says his figure drawing has to be better too. The worse of it is that he refuses to try oil painting, which almost certainly is the main barrier. Will, though more coarse in my opinion, is clever enough to appear polite and dresses up a little to please Academicians or would-be patrons. And of course he is wisely doing plenty of oil painting, though I still maintain his real gift is for watercolour.

Hannah says she thinks Tom is becoming more elegant in his manner and he certainly doesn't thrust his bad manners down people's throats, as Will does at times even now. I think about them too much in all probability, but it is because I do not want to think about Bethlem.

I need all the diversifying (diverting!) from my job I can get at the moment. The trouble is the board of governors have replaced the old apothecary at Bethlem with a man called John Haslam. He is from Edinburgh University, with an autocratic manner which I do not find attractive. He has already reversed Gozna's, the previous apothecary's, regime of using straight waistcoats, and prefers the use of chains to restrain the violent among the patients.

I pointed out when I first saw the chains that the straight waistcoat gave them more freedom around the hospital, but he maintained that the waistcoat was constricting and hot and didn't allow them to care for their own bodily functions. I had to agree with him that, with the shortage of servants to attend to them, this is an important consideration, but I do not like the chains and the chafing on the skin they promote. Chains puts one more in mind of a convict than a lunatic.

He and I do not agree about vomiting the patients either. He sees no point in it and he does not like the practice of dosing them with opium to calm them; it seems he would prefer them to be in chains if they show any violent tendencies. I am of the opinion, however, that opium calms and keeps them mellow.

I do not really want to spend my time quarrelling with him, and, as he is on the spot, there is not much I can do to stop him restraining them the way he wants to. All the same, I shall continue to vomit them and bathe them in the summer when it isn't so damnably cold there. What a site to build a hospital on! They say it was originally a marsh or river bed and the place is gradually sinking into it.

The whole Moorfields building, though imposing enough from the outside, needs repairing; the walls have draughts howling through the chinks and the roof leaks. It is the devil's own job to know where to start with all the governors saying we have not the money to do it, and as for the smell, it gets worse every year I declare. I often wonder how the lunatics survive.

1796

Tom was trailing far behind William's quick but steady pace on the Fetcham Road.

'Will, you know I cannot walk so fast as you! Slow down. I don't think I shall attempt this journey to the Doctor's ever again.'

'You mustn't give up now, Tom. Maybe we can get you a lift on a cart some of the way. I see it as the only way forward for us, me the son of a barber and you with your dad dying young like that, we have to meet rich art lovers among the gentry, don't you see?'

'It may be for you, you've already branched out into oils; but that is not for me. I must stay with watercolour.' Tom speeded up for a few paces and then fell behind a little again. 'I think I am unlikely to get into the Academy schools, so I have little hope of a bright future like you. My only hope is to marry money. Now I'm twenty I am going to spend all my efforts trying to procure a wife with money.'

Will stopped for a moment. 'Oh, Tom, you don't want to get involved seriously with women. That means you have to have them in the house cluttering it up with babies and things you don't want. Look at the good Doctor, whenever he talks of his wife and four children I sense a weariness. And that time we saw her she gave us a very queer look.'

'She has a squint, that's all. So how are you going to manage for women? Or is art going to be your mistress?

Don't tell me you're a celibate; I've seen you ogling the girls at the inns.'

'Oh, I shan't do without women, it's just marriage I don't particularly like the look of, seeing what my parents have made of it! My father may want to live with me some time soon anyway. He says either he or Mama will have to leave Maiden Lane sooner or later.'

'Wouldn't you have her to live with you if you get a place of your own?'

'No fear. Sometimes I feel sorry for her but usually I hate her. She has ungovernable rages and then both Father and I have to leave the house if we want to be safe. She's destroyed several of my pictures, for which I cannot, no, I will not forgive her. Luckily they weren't oils. I keep them hidden or she would do it for spite. I am always afraid she will discover my hiding place, so I change it frequently. She is malicious, Tom. My father only married her because her family had money. She was thirty-four when he married her, much older than him. She probably thought it was her last chance.' He laughed and wiped his mouth on his dirty sleeve. 'She wasn't too bad till my sister died, that was when I was eleven. I was sent away for a while and when I got back Mary Anne was gone. I don't think of her much now. She was always frail. Still I miss her. I would like to have a sister or brother, like you've got Tom.'

Girtin changed the subject, feeling an awkwardness. 'Why do you want to do oils, Will, aren't water colours what you excel in?'

'They may be now, but if you want to get on in the Academy you must paint in oils.'

'I am surprised, knowing you can show at the Academy, that you bother to walk all these dusty miles to Fetcham, on the off chance you can get the Doctor to introduce you to Angerstein.'

'I've told you: Locke is a big fish, but Angerstein is a

24

bigger one. You know he's got a huge collection of Claudes. I want to see them. The gentry buy Claudes, and I have to know his secret. I'm made if I get Angerstein interested, and what's more I am selfless enough to want my mate Tom to get some of the riches as they come raining down.' He nudged his friend, who grinned. 'Joseph Mallord William Turner, how does that sound?'

'Pretty stupid. Is that your name or are you going to adopt it?'

'It *is* my name. I'm called after my uncles on Mama's side, butchers in Brentford, doing well, but I shall be the one to immortalise the name.' He saw Tom's grimace. 'There are too many Turners around in the art world anyway; I know at least two. My three initials will make mine stand out. I'm no fool.'

'It's a bit of a mouthful, all the same. I think I'll stick with just plain Tom Girtin.'

At this Tom began to cough as a passing cart threw up its dust on the rutted road.

'Pray for rain, Joseph Mallord William! I cannot do with this dust; I always fear another attack and I think they grow worse. If it would only rain and settle the dust.' He coughed some more and tried to draw in his breath painfully. But Will had run on ahead and stopped the cart.

'Come on, Tom, he will take us to Dorking. We are in luck. Never trouble with the dust now.'

Tom sat happily dangling his legs from the slow-moving cart, while William fretted that he could actually walk faster than the horse.

'Go on, get down and run, then,' Tom said.

'I want to arrive not too covered in dust, especially if we are going to visit Norbury Park itself today.'

'Perhaps you should have brought some other clothes,' Tom suggested with a slight sneer.

'I have, but my hair will still be full of dust and I know

25

Monro won't let us upstairs to clean up. I shall have to change in a hedgerow.'

'Not many of the riches you talked of showering on you are likely to come my way. I don't have any clothes to change into.'

'Get yourself some and then get yourself a patron. Money is the key to everything, Tom. I don't mind working for it, but I don't believe in working to no end.'

'I told you, a rich woman is my way, that or giving lessons.'

'Oh, lessons, that's a drudge's way out.'

'All the same I've heard you say you've given lessons and charged highly for them, too.'

Will looked earnestly into his companion's face as they rounded a bend in the road and they saw at last the houses of Dorking. 'Tom, you have enormous talent and so have I. Why be modest about it, when we know? Don't hide your talent under a bushel. Let it see the light of day, ingratiate yourself with these stupid men, these bankers who think they know what good art is and want to buy up art to impress people with just how cultured they are. Be a businessman, not just an artist! Use people like Monro. He uses us!'

'This is as far as I can take you, masters.'

They jumped down as the cart wound its slow way into the town and the horse stopped at a trough to drink.

'Monro doesn't use us; I think he genuinely wants to help,' Tom said, trying out his stiff legs again.

'Balderdash!' Will Turner spat into the road to emphasise the word.

'He was kind when I had my attack, very kind in fact. Sent me home in his carriage.'

'Oh, he likes you, you're biddable. He thinks I'm vulgar and coarse, but I don't care. I shall spit and use coarse words in front of him and he'll have to put up with it

26

because he knows I'm a genius. In a few years he'll be boasting to his arty friends that he was the one who started Turner on his career!'

'I'm not biddable, Will, and I've seen you change your behaviour if you thought it suited a would-be patron.'

Will laughed. 'I might drop a few less h's if Angerstein comes along, but I know Monro will hold onto me however often I spit and I don't care if the wife won't receive me. What does she matter?'

Thomas's diary

I had made up my mind to write up my diary once a year, and as I started it with Turner and Girtin arriving, that seemed a good enough date to keep every year. However, I have a great need to write down some of my thoughts, largely about work, and this cannot wait. Somehow I cannot talk to Hannah about it, despite thinking when I married her that we would share everything. I now realise that it is not fair to burden her with problems which are perhaps mere clouds on the horizon and, if I am frank, I did not share these thoughts with her today because I am aware that she would not really be interested or understand. This is a sad admission, but the children have divided us; she is first and foremost a mother, and I'm . . . what am I first and foremost? An art lover? A father? A physician?

My disturbance stems from the fact that a new sort of asylum has been opened for the insane in York; it is known as the York Retreat, and as its name hints, it is more caring than Bedlam, as the press point out (they always use the slang name for it, of course). The Governors are concerned at the crude comparisons being drawn between our establishment and this one. For instance, they have lady visitors in York. We of course no longer allow anyone to visit, or

27

rather to gawp, which is roughly what the crowds used to do. The meeting of the Board of Governors was stormy; some saying we must reform, others complaining, as they always do, that our staff do not carry out their duties properly – not meaning me or Haslam, thank the Lord, but the underlings who actually deal physically with the inmates. The arguments always end up the same way: lack of funds. If you pay so little you get the dregs of society to work for you.

Haslam shrugs his shoulders at the skiving off, the drunkenness, the petty stashing away of food meant for the inmates that ends up in the mouths of the staff. 'You get what you pay for,' he says. I privately agree, but I have to try and stir him up to greater efforts every time we meet.

I used to bless the day when my father agreed to let me succeed him and my grandfather as Bethlem Physician. I was not the eldest, my brother John was, and he died young. I saw my chance and took it before my siblings really realised they could have asked first. I'm not sure that Charles, who was next eldest, ever really forgave me that, though we have never spoken of it directly.

But now I often think Charles could have the job with my blessing. Of course I only think that when I am depressed or worried that there will be repercussions, as I do now. Mostly I remember that Bethlem gives me a good income and a name in the profession.

I know if I resigned, the private madhouses would not really be adequate for my income or my reputation. They are not trouble-free either, of course. I have recently had problems with a man named Belcher. I tried to help the man because he seemed to be sane enough to be discharged from my Hackney madhouse. He most ungratefully then wrote a pamphlet which included a public letter to me and, though I should I suppose be grateful to him for calling me a man of feeling and understanding, the gist of it was that it is the *sane* who are often confined in madhouses, but go

28

rapidly mad after putting up with the other mad people they encounter there! I am glad to say the pamphlet did not get much publicity.

I have to agree in private that Belcher may have had a point, however, though sometimes they can learn from seeing other people madder than themselves. It depends on the kind of madness they show. I had the sense not to tell Hannah about Belcher's pamphlet, as she would have been outraged for me.

I have to admit a reluctant interest in the whole subject, almost despite myself. After all I went into it for the money and security, not because the subject of madness fascinated me when I was young. For instance I've recently enjoyed reading of a case of matricide by a lunatic, one Mary Lamb. She has gone to Fisher House in Islington and is not to stand trial. Apparently she worked at home as a seamstress but also cared for an infirm mother and elderly father. One fateful day her apprentice girl annoyed her and Mary was running after her to harm her when the mother intervened, whereat she stabbed her own mother. One of the Board of Governors asked me privately whether I would not have preferred to see her hung or at least put in Bethlem.

'Well,' I replied, 'if they do not hang Margaret Nicholson for trying to stab the King, then why should they hang this woman who, it seems had in all other ways been a model offspring, doing her best and set about with poverty as well as with difficult parents? If a relative can afford it, she is better in a private madhouse than in Bethlem.'

His only answer was that I was not speaking up well for my own hospital! I think Father gave me his blessing even though I was not next in line to 'inherit' Bethlem, partly because we shared a love of art, even though I ignored his suggestion that I should try and go abroad as he had, and learn from the Italian masters. They never appealed and I still can't understand all these wealthy men like Angerstein and Hoare and Beckford wanting to buy Claudes. Gainsborough far outdoes him in sensitivity, and he is English! It is merely fashion that dictates their taste in art, I fear.

I had an argument with Will Turner the other day about Wilson, such an Italian in his approach, whom he still maintains is the greatest of English landscapists, apart from himself of course.

Reading this back to myself I realise I have left the subject of madhouses far behind and reverted to my favourite subject, art. Well, so be it.

I was amazed to see the lads back with me this winter, but of course they must feel indebted for the connections they have made through me. Or rather, William has made. I fear Tom is not, for all his charm, prepared to push himself in the right direction, nor will he adapt to the Academy style. I went to the lengths of commissioning three pictures when he embarked on his first independent tour ever, this year. These were to be views of Jedburgh, York and Durham Cathedrals, which Girtin executed for me. They cost me 4 guineas each and I am proud to possess them, but the disparity between Will and Tom's careers so far still worries me.

Hannah was amazed when I got her to come with me to see the new Academy's exhibition. After all it is only a few yards down the road to Somerset House, so she cannot complain of fatigue. Thank God her health does seem to have improved, after a bad spell following Sally's birth which worried me a good deal at the time. I think the air of Fetcham for the second summer running has helped her.

We went partly to see *Fisherman at sea* on the Academy walls, Will's first big oil painting.

'Is that *our* Mr Turner?' she said, and when I told her yes, she kept going back across the room to it. 'Can that be painted by the one who spits and can't eat without dropping bits on the floor? Look at the way he's got the moonlight

30

on the water, and you can really feel the oily swell on the waves!'

'Talent doesn't always come accompanied with good manners, more's the pity,' I told her, dryly.

Then when we read the revues, which of course William thrust under our noses ('in possession of genius and judgement' one said) she was even more amazed. She even said as we went to bed one night, 'Perhaps you have been very clever, Thomas.'

'What do you mean, in what respect?' I asked, watching her disrobe. She had been petitioning me to buy her a new-style dress, with a high waist, and I have to admit she looks good in it, now she has got one. It is pink with little bunches of flowers on it. I would even go as far as to say she looks charming in it, despite the weight she has put on with four confinements.

'In gaining some sketches and pictures by that Will Turner,' she answered. 'Maybe he will be famous just as he says he will be. But he doesn't deserve to be. Now that nice Tom Girtin, *he* deserves it. Did you hear someone bought Will's *Fishermen at sea* for ten guineas? When I heard that, I wished it was Tom who'd sold something for that sort of money.'

For nowadays Hannah does dare to come down and see the lads when they are with me on Friday evenings. This is the third year they have come and I wonder if we shall see a fourth, and so I told her. As to Tom Girtin, I'm very afraid his health and his lack of ambition will hold him back. Farington has failed to get him into the Academy schools and he always seems short of money, so he does not look respectable when he does meet people like Hoppner who might be helpful to him.

'Well, I prefer his modesty to that William Turner's inflated sense of himself. When I think that you rescued him from a cellar in Maiden Lane . . .'

'Hardly true, my dear, but I think you are right. I may have been cleverer than I realised. At least when I die, our four children may have some patrimony, if Turner continues to make a name for himself as he is doing at present.'

'Don't talk of dying, Tom. What a loss you would be to all the lunatics as well as to the art world,' and she laughed, because she loves to tease me.

I am not so sure that Tom Girtin is really modesty personified as Hannah sees him. It is only beside his friend William that he appears so.

William has been ill this winter and we saw more of Tom. I had not expected that vigorous little fellow to fall ill, but he has been working overtime to get his *Fishermen at sea* ready for the Academy show. Tom is not really well either but he comes more often this winter all the same.

I felt happy because I was able through Hoppner to get him introduced to Lascelles, and immediately I felt that there was a rapport between him and Tom Girtin, I was almost glad that William was absent that night. Lascelles has a great deal of money and sway.

But of course William did meet Lascelles (he wouldn't miss a trick), and both lads benefited from the connection. From what I gather, Lascelles took to Tom's impulsive and vigorous ways and his modesty, whereas he respects William's art, rather than his personality.

Now Hannah is calling and I see my clock says half past eleven. I feel somewhat clearer in the head, though all that I can see before me is the necessity at the next meeting of the Governors to tell them yet again they must use any funds they can raise to provide more latrines and clean water at Bethlem. We will have to take our chance in comparisons with York asylum.

*

32

Thomas Monro is seated on a bench under a large beech tree, with the Green Man, a small inn, behind him. He is on a journey between Brooke House in the village of Hackney, one of his private mental homes, and his newly acquired country house in Surrey, near Dorking.

His air is weary, although he has paper and pencil in front of him and is endeavouring to represent the smiling scene before him, made up of a sparkling lake or large pond, with a bridge across one end of it, and trees growing to the side of it up a bank. Cows graze serenely beside it.

His horse, Brandy, is tied to the hitching post beside the inn, trying to reach some of the leaves of a bush nearby, after eating any grass he could find between the paving stones of the courtyard. After a few curious glances, the landlord and servant girl have gone indoors, away from the heat of the sun, leaving their guest to sit alone and pursue his hobby undisturbed. The whole area sleeps.

The water of the pond is something he has chosen as a subject, to wash away, as it were, some of the depression and frenzy of the madhouse he is in charge of, and which, whether he likes it or not, fills his thoughts.

His manager Holmes runs Brooke House well, but it is Thomas's job to decide on the treatment of the mad people in his charge and quite often he is puzzled indeed as to how to go about it.

He has long been of the opinion that management of the insane is better than medicine. He keeps his patients secluded, though at certain times of day they do mix with each other, as much to learn from each other's follies as anything else. Diet is also important, and here he and Holmes do not always agree.

Thomas is busy wondering, as he shades in his trees and wipes his brow, for it is hot even under the tree, what he should do with a new, potentially violent patient who today would only weep when spoken to.

Certainly a diet of bread and milk would be better than the cheese and porter given to her so far by Holmes. The man's defence was that that was what she had requested and as she was a Lord's daughter, he had done her bidding.

Thomas had been peremptory with him about kow-towing to the aristocracy when dealing with their relatives. 'Her father is not going to bless you for giving her meals which make her behaviour more violent.' Thomas had seen this sort of behaviour in a woman before, weeping and washing her hands all the time, and was gloomy as to whether the woman would recover her wits. He knew that she grieved partly for a baby who had died, but there was no treatment for grief that he knew of, except patient understanding.

He had suggested she might be given some basic needle-work to give her rest for her mind, as well as some carefully chosen books, but Holmes had objected that she had torn up the only book he had tried so far and had pricked her wrists with the needle. Luckily, Holmes grimly added, someone had seen her do this before she got too far and drew too much blood.

Thus it was hard to think what one could give her to do which was safe. He gave up and suggested that controlled bleeding of the patient by an apothecary might help to calm her. Holmes agreed.

Thomas had also been worried that the place smelled, and although Bethlem always smelled, he had always prided himself that Brooke House did not and that the close stools were always washed out thoroughly twice a day.

Holmes had explained that several of the patients had defecated on the floor and then started to spread it over the walls early that morning. That was why the smell that day was worse, although of course he had seen to it that it was cleaned up very carefully.

34

Holmes was obviously doing his best, but visitors like the father of Lucinda Darlby would not take kindly to that sort of smell lingering about the place. This he had explained to Holmes, who had agreed with him and had gone on to say that it would not happen again.

Thomas had wondered then, and still wondered, how Holmes would disallow it, given that rational explanation or punishment did not always work on deranged minds.

However, what had wearied him the most that morning had really not been to do with the imbeciles, but a swarm of bees that had landed in a tree near one of the windows of Brooke House. The man who was supposed to deal with it had not come and Thomas had stupidly let himself get stung by getting too near to see what he could do himself. Then one of the inmates had come near the window and taken fright, howling and screaming, which had upset the rest of them. Well, at least, he remembered wryly, by the time they had been calmed down again, his sting was hurting a good deal less, and now, thank goodness, not at all.

He noticed with slight irritation, as he looked up, that the two cowherds or labourers of some sort who had lately passed him with a 'Goo' afternoon', were sitting by the pond, wasting their time most probably in idle chat. However, they might be included in the picture, as only the top of their heads really showed above the bank, and thus were easier to draw than full figures, over which he had trouble as a rule.

By the time he had included them and made a huge effort to represent the reflections in the pond, he noticed the light was softer and, getting out his watch, saw it was already five o'clock and that he must be riding on. His horse was moving restlessly, as much as to say, 'You know Hannah and the children will be waiting.'

But as he put his sketch book and pens in his saddlebag, he realised how much more rested he felt about Brooke

House and Lucinda Darlby, even though he had the much worse task tomorrow of riding into Moorfields, to Bethlem and its stench, not to mention Mr Haslam, who was certainly not as reasonable nor as efficient as Holmes. The two labourers he had added to his sketch at the last moment were in fact, he also realised, an asset to the picture.

'Thank God for my hobby,' he thought as he swung his leg over the horse's back and trotted briskly out of the inn yard.

1797

Thomas's diary

As usual I write on the anniversary of the lads' arrival, though this year they have outgrown me in no uncertain terms. They, are in fact, at Harewood in Yorkshire, working for Lascelles in his own abode. I hear from Lascelles himself that both lads have sketched a place called Plompton Rocks on the estate. He tells me he prefers Girtin, just as I do and Hannah too; but that he thinks Turner is probably going to make more of a name for himself. Turner he has asked to paint an oil landscape to fit a certain space in his library, but Girtin he has taken on as his drawing master. There is some gossip that Girtin has been wild in the taverns around the estate and that this has injured his association with Lascelles, but I don't think this rumour can be true if he still takes Tom Girtin to be his art tutor.

Cozens, as I feared, has died without recovering his sanity and his sketches are up for sale. Holmes has for some months predicted he could not last much longer; he was raving all summer. I did not see the man when sane and I do not feel any real sadness at his departure. I shall see whether I can afford the prices, as his death has given him a notoriety he did not possess earlier. Beckford, I hear, did not attend the funeral but Beaumont and Payne Knight did. I suspect Beckford and Cozens had quarrelled, and I was told that Beckford only took on Cozens as his official artist on the Grand Tour to please his father, Alexander Cozens, whom Beckford liked.

I had in fact bought Alexander's book when I was a lad; he had some novel ideas about how to create bushes in landscapes by means of blotches! I think it helped free up my style a little when I tried his theories out, but on the whole I would not follow them. Beaumont asked me to go to the funeral but I was not able to, owing to a prior engagement. I felt a little that I had been expected to cure him, but those people who thought so are not really aware of the complications of insanity. Our King went mad in the same way, a few years ago, but in that case mercifully recovered without any particular reason, so I fear there is a long way to go before we understand the workings of the diseased mind.

We see Turner when he thinks there is someone here who would interest him. He does sometimes work with Girtin as before, but it is getting less usual as an occurrence. Hannah always goes upstairs if she thinks William Turner is dining; she cannot bear his manners, which have not improved, even though his fame has. It is as if he is daring the world, Take me as I am or not at all! I cannot help thinking that if he dines with any of his richer patrons he does make more effort, which is not a comfortable thought. I must be quite a long way down the line, if the manners he adopts in Adelphi Terrace are anything to go by!

Girtin has begun a venture which I fear is a stupid one and will not be good for his health. A wealthy cloth manufacturer by the name of Hayward has agreed to let him use his warehouse to paint a huge circular panorama of London which he plans to call the Eidometropolis. What a name! He is busy sketching London from the roof of some factory in Southwark, near where he was born; then he will transfer it into oils in seven large sections. He plans it to be 200 feet long, but when I told Hannah she stared and said that was impossible. She fears the dusty and draughty warehouse is no place for Girtin to spend his days. She thinks he has consumption. I gather his father died young from a sort of cough and breathlessness. Maybe Tom has the same disease, but personally I do not think it is consumption.

He got the idea for the Eidometropolis when the Barkers made their huge panorama to rival Loutherberg's Eidophusikon. Theirs was 10,000 square feet but I did not visit it. I somehow feel Tom has taken the wrong turning. The public will easily tire of this sort of thing, which is more a kind of theatre than real art. I advised him against it, but he said he could not, like Turner, please the Academy by doing oil paintings. He must be true to his own genius.

I couldn't help but laugh when I was telling Hannah the other night about one of our lunatics just admitted. His name is James Tilly Matthews. Here we have the real French spy that everyone always says Tom Girtin is! Haslam maintains Matthews is not one, but the man has been in prison in Paris for trying to negotiate peace with the Girondists, for the last five years or so, and now he is declared mad and been sent to us. I find it hard to say whether he is really insane, but there never has been any sure-fire test of sanity, of course. I fear he may be a trouble maker; he is obviously intelligent and not your run-of-the-mill lunatic. He has already complained of the cold and the food! I have never eaten the food but I certainly have experienced the cold.

1799

Thomas's diary

I miss the lads, although I do see Tom from time to time. I
gather he has moved twice in the last two years, endeavouring to find a good cheap room near the centre of town.
When I met him first he lived in St Martin's-le-Grand, from
the window of which he sketched St Paul's. We hear much
of William. Farington told me grimly that William had
pointedly told him that he had been offered 40 guineas by
Angerstein, for a watercolour of Carnaervon Castle! He
also dropped into that conversation the fact that Colt Hoare
wants him to do more views of Salisbury cathedral and that
Beckford has invited him to that extraordinary folly of a
place of his, Fonthill, to work there. Apparently Beckford
even wrote all the way from Portugal to ask him.

'Turner is trying to bully me into getting him elected
ARA,' said Farington. 'He lost out last year, just when he
thought it was in the bag. The second ballot went against
him; Shee and Rossi got in instead. You have to hand it to
him for his single-mindedness! He'll do it next time if the
amount of hectoring and persuasion he has brought to bear
on everyone I know counts for anything. I don't like him
but I admire his cheek.

'You know he has given me and several other people on
the committee some of his work,' Farington went on. 'We
went to Maiden Lane and chose what we wanted. He is
singular in that he calls the pictures he does his "children".
I was amused but not for long. What a place that is. I mean

40

his home. I must say I felt for him when I heard his mother shouting at his father through the wall. It sounded like a wild beast, not a human being. I thought she might burst through and start attacking me!'

Farington apparently advised Will not to move away altogether until he had several hundred pounds behind him, because Will asked him if he thought it a good idea to reside at a more respectable address as soon as he could get one. I said I didn't suppose it would take him that long to accrue the sort of money he needs, as has been proved to be the case.

I have decided to stick all my Turner works into a special album. I think this is something I can show off to friends now that he is attracting so much attention. Beaumont, however, rather to my surprise, does not like him and runs him down to anyone he meets. He much prefers Girtin's style, which some say is unfinished, and Lascelles is trying to get Girtin in to the RA instead of William. He is still having lessons from Tom and says what a fine fellow he is. Though he buys pictures from Turner he says he has no respect for him as a man! I agreed with him but laughed to think that all the same every one of them pored over my album. How unfair it is that the good Lord gave Will so much talent.

Girtin went to Wales with Lascelles and I hear that the latter has bought two of the scenes Girtin did there. I have seen a very amusing picture Girtin did in Bettws y Coed, it is of a bridge and below on the rocks a poor artist has lost his hat and is trying without success to get it back before it hits the water. It amused Hannah a good deal and everyone I know who has seen it is rather charmed than dismissive of the wit he has used there. On a more serious note I have heard that Girtin has refused rather a lucrative offer from Lord Elgin who goes soon as ambassador to Turkey. I think Turner was offered the job too, but he is doing too well to be tempted. Lady Elgin wished Girtin to accompany her to Turkey and teach her, but he says he is no lady's man, scraping and bowing and teaching someone with no talent to paint fire screens! He says 30 guineas a year is not enough to tempt him. Girtin is no lackey and I rather respect him for the decision, but it would have been a sinecure compared with painting his Eidometropolis. Also the climate might have suited him better.

But Farington told me that Girtin was very angry at being treated like some tradesman, kicking his heels outside Lord Elgin's door, and then being offered less a year than he pays his *valet-de-chambre*! It was that that really put him off.

There is one thing I have done that I must write about. It does not please me when I think about it. Thank God I did not tell Hannah of it, and long may she live in ignorance of my part in it. It is to do with William Turner's mother.

Although I had not seen Will so much in the last year, he suddenly came out of the blue to see me this very evening. His father, the last time I had my hair cut, had informed me his wife was getting worse and he did not know which way he could turn. He gave me rather a speaking glance as he said it and I realised that something was afoot even then. It turned out that he and William wanted me to get her into Bethlem, by saying that she had never been a danger to others, which of course I know isn't true, and also that she is poor and therefore must be an object of charity.

'But surely,' I said, 'you would want her to be a private patient. I could find room, I am fairly certain, for her in one of my homes for the insane. There is Brooke House, and I have another in Clerkenwell.'

William, to do him some justice, looked uncomfortable.

'We cannot afford it, and she must go to Bethlem if you will help us. I know there is a waiting list, but with your help we can get her in without waiting.'

'Do you really mean that you cannot afford to send her somewhere else?' I peered at him closely.

Turner grew angry and very fidgety at this. 'It is none of your business what I do with my money and my father is certainly too poor to pay.' I doubted that too, as he has always been a clever and efficient barber.

There was a silence, a long one, and finally I reluctantly picked up my pen and did what he wanted, but I am not happy that I did it. I managed to get the poor woman into St Luke's. She will go from there to Bethlem I presume, unless the father and son decide to move her to Brooke House. I offered them a place at any time and told them the terms, but the man who 'could not afford it' is the same one who moved to a fashionable address and that is why I suspect the money is not available. To crown it all, this time round, since I began to write this entry, he got his way and become ARA, through much wheeling and dealing with anyone he can get to hear his case, not just Farington.

I feel very mixed; proud that I have helped a man obviously destined for a great career, if he can do all this before he is even 25; but also unhappy that such a sly, coarse, avaricious brute should achieve greater things than Tom Girtin, who seems to have so much better qualities and is not far behind Turner as a painter. Yes, I would stick my neck out and say that.

I wonder if Turner remained friends longer with me than was necessary to his career just because he knew I could help over his mother. I remember now when I first asked Will to come to Adelphi Terrace how he hung back and how his father mentioned my job and my connexion with Bethlem. It's an uncomfortable thought that he might have agreed to come only so that he could get his mother into a lunatic asylum if she grew worse. I did think of changing my barber, but unless I am also prepared never to see the son again, it is a paltry gesture. He is also a very good barber.

For all these reasons I am very glad to have the new lad Cotman, although Hannah sighed and said she had thought I had got taking on uncouth lads out of my system. He turned up one evening, rang the bell and the servant turned him away. However, he came back, and this time I happened to be near the door and heard him ask for the Doctor, so I signalled to the servant to let him come into the hall and I had a look at him by the light of a candle or two. There was something about him that appealed to me and when he said that he had been told that I helped struggling young artists, I couldn't help thinking, why not a third?

He comes from Norwich and managed to get a job with Ackermann the print seller, but now he has started to do some copying I can see that he and Ackermann may not last long together. He is not a very biddable lad, indeed he is a strange mixture of self-importance and awkward lack of confidence. His accent is so difficult to understand that I had to ask him what he said several times over. He winced when I did it more than twice. He was not afraid to comment on one of the pictures that hangs in my hall, but I still am not sure what he said about it! That was the first time he called. Now I am getting a little better at understanding him. He often gestures with his thumb towards something on the wall and makes a not always very kind comment. I try to ignore this, after all he is only 16 and probably wanting to impress.

I have also started to encourage a man called John Varley, or rather two brothers, Cornelius and John Varley. They, too, came to see me but had been recommended before they arrived through a contact in the art world, so I was more than happy to receive them and thought they could make up a threesome of a winter evening in my house, as Girtin and Turner did. John is a big lad, warm and a good artist as far as I can tell. He is a nice change from Cotman, who is awkward and invariably takes up what

44

I say wrongly. As I said, I think he lacks confidence, though it emerges as cantankerousness at times. Cornelius has not made a very good impression as yet. First he let drop that he knows Girtin well. Then he added that Tom had told him he was not very happy at having been restricted to drawing when he was with me.

All three have been out to Fetcham and have been sketching with me. What pleasure it gives me to help these young men, especially John Varley.

*

Tom Girtin was standing on the muddy strand of the Thames looking up at the lighted windows of the Doctor's house, when he saw William Turner coming out of the door.

Their greeting was colder than it had been even a year earlier.

'So what are you doing skulking about outside the "good" Doctor's?' Turner asked.

'Wondering whether to go in. What were *you* doing? Not copying more Cozens or Hearnes I imagine.'

'No, not that it's your business.'

There was a pause while Tom shuffled his feet and nudged a piece of driftwood into the tiny wavelet at the edge of the water. The rumble of carts came from the bridge downstream.

'I was actually wondering whether to ask him to help me as a doctor.'

'Are you worse, then?' Turner's tone sounded less sneering, and he looked at Girtin closely.

'Certainly no better. I don't think London agrees with me, but I'm bent on doing this panorama, though Hayward and I have quarrelled, which makes things more difficult.'

'I heard about it. And you still give lessons to Lascelles?'

'Sometimes. I gather he has bought several more of your pieces.'

45

'Oh yes, he buys, but he likes you better. Stupid Tory. Give me Fawkes any time.'

'It's Lascelles's brother who stood as a Tory up in York- shire, and well you know it, Will.'

'I can't understand you, Tom. You continue to sport that Jacobin haircut, which hasn't done you any good with people like Hoppner and Farington, and yet you support Tories against Whigs like Fawkes. And Fawkes is a demo- crat. He doesn't look down on me for my crude ways as I'm sure the good Doctor would call them. He welcomes me to Farnley Hall. He never puts on airs.'

'I don't support Lascelles's politics, I get on with him as a person. In any case I don't want to be drawn into who should win an election, his brother or Fawkes. I wish you joy of Fawkes, so perhaps in your turn you could find it in your heart to wish me joy of teaching Lascelles.'

Something in his tone seemed to reach the other man. 'I do, Tom. I have no ambitions there. And what's your news otherwise?'

He came and crouched beside Tom at the water's edge, picked up a pebble and threw it into the water. 'Look at the way the lights are reflected on the water and the shadows under the bridge. What a lot there is still to learn in painting.'

'Mmm. I've actually been painting the river a lot; not at this level, but from above with all its buildings, wharves and boats . . . it's good. You probably know the Barkers' patent on panoramas is running out and I think I can better their efforts.' He fidgeted a little. 'I've also been courting a rich woman. Her father, Phineas Borret, owns quite a lot of property in Essex.'

'Aha. Your future is made then?'

'Maybe, but I also love her, that's really the point.'

'Indeed?' and he laughed up into Tom's face.

'I hear you are seeing quite a bit of Mrs Danby now her husband is dead. Be careful, she has three girls already I'm told and another child on the way. Poor woman, but don't forget you said you'd never be cluttered up with domesticity.'

'Nor shall I. Yes, I am seeing her, as you put it. She says I'm more fun in bed than her husband was; he was quite an old man.' He saw Tom Girtin blush at his directness and added, 'All the same I miss him and his music. I took up the flute, you know, under his urgings. I'm not that good but it was fun when we all sang and played together. But don't mistake me; I visited them when he was alive and I still visit rather than live there. I shall buy my own place soon. I shall always need my own place, with no interference from anyone. Women are all right, but in their place and that's usually bed! Wilson had the right idea, he never married; he had a by-blow though, at least one or maybe more. It's not so uncommon.'

There was a silence; the two men both watching a sailing barge drift downstream with its brown sails against the blackness of the night.

'Lucky Monro,' Tom said. 'With this place right on the river and the place at Fetcham for the months when London gets hot and unpleasant.'

'He deserves it, no doubt,' William said unexpectedly. 'Mad people are no fun.'

'How's your mother?'

'Oh, the same. Monro's going to admit her to Bedlam in fact.'

'Whew!' Tom whistled but had the sense not to enquire further, from the stubborn yet anguished look that had appeared on William's face, an expression he had never seen there before.

'What about *your* work, apart from the Eidometropolis!'

47

'I shall go to Wales with Beaumont next year, I think. He is generous and only needs help with his sketches *now and again.*' Girtin laughed.

'Yes, at least Monro never asks us to help him and he isn't a bad artist. Limited but knows it. Beaumont thinks he's no end of a swell as an artist. He can't stand me, as you probably know. Jealous, I suppose. Sounds funny when he's a Sir and owns millions. He speaks against me whenever he can, but so far he hasn't harmed me with anyone that counts, as far as I can work out.'

Tom let the remark about jealousy rest. 'They say you're getting interested in poetry, that you write it even. Is that true?'

'Yes, I've been reading Thomson. He says just what I feel. I would be happy to write like him. I know I started with a poor education but I am not going to let that get in my way. I intend to write as well as anyone else and of course paint better than anyone else.' He laughed. 'I'm going to use poetry when I show my work, in the catalogue, to make one echo the other. You know what Reynolds said about poetry being able to explain and describe a whole scene, but a picture only being able to show one moment. I think that it's a good idea to use both when one can; I hope to write my own verse, or I might use a famous poet like Thomson, or Milton even. Would you like to hear some of my poetry?'

There was obviously something in his companion's face because he went on, 'I started by writing glees, you know like Danby did; then I realised I could write in Thomson's style or Milton's even!'

He laughed, but Girtin said hurriedly, 'Let me tell you my news before you start spouting your verses. I'm also starting a new venture. With a few friends. I don't know if you know Francia, he's a French refugee.'

48

'Oh no, not the old sympathies rearing up, Tom?' Will rolled his eyes.

'Francia came over from France as a child. I'm no Jacobin and neither's he. He teaches at Barry's art school. He's a bit of a show-off, he can act the clumsy oaf, but he's a good fellow. Then there's Underwood, do you know him?'

'No, should I? In any case, what's the venture?'

'Seven of us have started a sort of drawing, sketching club, in our own homes. There's Francia, Underwood, me, Ker Porter, Denham, Samuel and Worthington.'

'I know Ker Porter, we used to fool around in the Academy schools with Henry Barker too. The tricks we used to play on old Wilton, the keeper there! Does Ker Porter still fool around?'

Tom shrugged. 'Not that I've noticed; he's a good chap and gifted. He won the Silver Palette at the Academy for his history painting, he told me. We meet each Saturday evening at each other's houses in turn and that week's host suggests a motif for the night, usually taken from a poem. Then we all draw it and the host, or what we call the President of the Night, keeps the sketches. We each provide some porter and a bite to eat when it is our turn. It lasts from seven till midnight.'

'Sounds like Monro's all over again. Not that we ever got a drop of porter up there though,' and he gestured towards the house. 'I don't think I would care to repeat the experience, even with the porter thrown in!'

If Girtin was disappointed that Turner showed little interest in his club he took care not to show it. 'We never got the freedom to draw what we wanted, did we? Draw was the operative word for me, he never let me near the colours!'

'That still rankles, doesn't it? You should bless him, it probably kept you on the straight and narrow.'

49

'What's that supposed to mean?'

'Oh, nothing. So what do you call yourselves, your new group?'

'The Brothers.'

'Brothers! Ha! so you *are* a covert Jacobin. I like it, I like it a lot.'

'I'm glad you're so enthusiastic. Actually Francia chose it, not me.' Tom's sarcasm was lost in a bout of coughing. He got up from crouching and turned towards the houses behind him.

'I'm going in to see Monro just as I intended. He can only say no.' But he sounded rather unsure of himself.

'Are you short of cash, Tom? Do you want some help?'

Tom stared but shook his head. This was unheard of in William and he felt the kindness. Thus he took Will's hand for a second before turning away from the Doctor's house, still coughing. Perhaps he should take up Turner's offer of money and not bother the Doctor tonight.

Thomas's diary

I find so much is happening in the art world around me that I must break my self-made rule to write only once a year and add another entry regarding Girtin. What happened was this.

I was sitting gloomily over the Bethlem papers in my study one winter's evening, when Girtin was announced. It had been a terrible day; at the committee meeting I had tried to push through better sanitation rules and more privies for the decaying building we still are forced to use in Moorfields. I think the new well I have been urging on the Governors will come; but at the moment the lack of clean water and the state of the privies means disease is running riot, so they don't have much alternative but to get some

50

repairs done. I nearly threw up my post over all this, they are so grudging and they spend hours talk, talk, talking and getting nowhere, but then when I had practically given up on them, sanity prevailed.

The trouble is that quite apart from my salary, I am well known in the medical world as Chief Physician of Bethlem, and after all Haslam takes most of the brunt of it, as he should, living there all the time. It is his fault largely that the warders drink on the job. He will not listen if I talk of instituting inspections as they come in and out. He says you need the alcohol to keep you warm, it's so cold in there.

I'm sure he drinks too but is better able to disguise it, being a gentleman. When, oh when, will we move to better accommodation? Each Governors' meeting it is raised and nothing ever seems to happen. Well it is my cross. I must bear it until Tom comes to take over and I am past it.

Girtin was coughing badly but I was glad to see him. I wondered what he had come for, but I was startled by what he said. He asked pathetically if I could cure him and mentioned money. I was hesitant to say I did not really know of a cure, nor do I really think it is consumption, but something worse and equally incurable. I did say that my practice in curing the sick was rusty since I had been attempting to cure men's minds for most of my practising life as a doctor. However, I offered to get a colleague to have a look at him, and he was grateful. Again he mentioned money, but I gestured at the walls of my study where I have his best work hung; copies, but not really copies, of Cozens's work in the Alps and various later works that I have got from him. 'These are my payment,' I said.

He looked pleased.

'While you're here, I have someone you must meet,' I said, and I took him into the other room where Cotman was standing shyly listening to the conversation of my friends Hearne and Farington, who were standing over the fireplace, keeping the heat well to themselves. I had left them reluctantly earlier in the evening, because of Bethlem business.

I introduced them. 'Jack Cotman, Tom Girtin,' and I suggested Girtin take the lad, now I realise quite a lot younger than him, for Tom must be 24 at least and Jack only 16, into my study to show him his own sketches from Cozens.

Jack Cotman has talent, in my opinion, though Hannah laughs and says, 'Thomas, Thomas, all your geese are swans.'

'Well,' I said, 'one goose has turned into a very powerful swan indeed. You have to admit that.' A good analogy I thought afterwards: swans can be fierce; they can break your hand with one swipe of their wing apparently, and I would say the same of Turner. If you let him.

Cotman is not all that easy, in fact; he is awkward, difficult to please, unsure of himself still. I thought I'd had two difficult pupils, if that's what I should call them, already in Girtin and Turner, but he is more so. He is very provincial as yet but very eager to get on. Jack Cotman is impatient.

I like his watercolour style but I don't think it is a style that anyone else will take kindly to, outside the art world that is. It is very individualistic. With luck he will modify it. It would do no harm for him to imitate Cozens's style or Girtin's, come to think of it. However, so far he does not seem to have altered his own style one jot.

I was pleased later to find the two lads in the study talking nineteen to the dozen and Cotman saying, 'And you really mean I can join your Brothers?' as he leant over the table. Its one candle lit up his eager features at the same time as poor Girtin's unhealthy pallor.

'What's this?' I said jovially. 'Brothers?'

Tom blushed a little. 'William Turner laughed at the

name so I didn't tell you, sir, but I have started a sort of artists' club with four or five others. A little on the lines of what you have done for me and William.'

'It sounds very democratic,' I joked and he blushed again, but I was secretly pleased with the tribute he paid me, and also that these two had met under my roof. Although Hannah calls it meddling in people's lives, I think I *can* help these struggling young artists and have already done so. Even William Turner has to admit that.

I think Hannah calls it meddling because she is a little jealous of my 'lads'. 'You have your own lads growing up now,' she said to me. 'They should be your concern, not these artistic strangers.'

It is true; Tom is already ten and even Sally is five. Henry is still keen on drawing and Hannah thinks I spoil him with too much of my attention and ignore the others. Not true, I say.

I am 40 this year. It hit me the other day that I am more than half-way through my life with all probability. I have a lot to thank God for but I should like to go on using what influence I have to help others more gifted than myself and, selfishly, to talk art not only with men of my own age, but with the young, who are so fresh and see with a naive eye, assuredly, but with a fresh eye too.

I would rather talk with Varley and Cotman any day than with Farington, that gossip, and Beaumont, who pontificates. I don't count Hearne, even though he is getting an old chap these days, or Edridge, whom I've been seeing more of lately. He is such a successful portraitist and always the life and soul of the party. These are my real friends in any case.

Cotman was asking Girtin about Turner. Tom Girtin was nicer than I expected him to be about his old friend. I knew they had quarrelled over Lascelles and were drifting ever further apart as William became richer and more famous and Girtin iller, struggling with his Eidometropolis, and forced into teaching to keep enough money in his purse. Turner does not like it that Beaumont prefers Girtin and encourages his style. He is not used to having Girtin as a serious rival any more, but Beaumont and Lascelles are quite powerful in the art world.

I did not know then that Tom was courting a goldsmith's daughter in Islington. Smart move, I thought when I heard. I, too, should have married a rich woman, instead of sweating out my guts twice a week at Bethlem and coping with the mad gentry in my private homes, who at least do not stink like the ones in Bethlem. Of course Hannah as a girl was very winsome and respectable, despite her sister's history. It is hard to believe that she, a respectable vicar's daughter from Watford, somehow became the Kings' mistress for a while. Poor Hannah, she never has quite lived Sarah down. I think this great stress she puts on respectability in our lives must stem from that. She will never really explain how it came about and I think the family have tried to keep it a secret.

She told me just the other day, 'I put up with William Turner and I came to like Tom, but that's enough. I am not coming to meet any further protégés. Your Varleys and your Cotmans can remain yours. I shall be upstairs in my sitting room or in the nursery, but I do take it unkindly that you cannot spend more time with our Tom who is much in need of a father now as he outgrows the nursery.' So it ended up that I promised her I would spend more time with the elder boys.

54

1800

Tom Girtin is sitting with the Brothers in Francia's lodgings, but it is for the last time. He is getting married the following day and knows his wife will expect, at least at first, that he spend more time with her than with artists.

Cotman is now a Brother and a frank admirer of the older man.

'That is a wonderful tree you have drawn, Tom. It really has a bewitched look under the moon, and those clouds and shadows! I wish you would not leave. I don't feel at ease with the others as yet.'

'You'll be fine; they are good fellows and after all, are we not all "brothers"?' He patted Cotman on the back, laughed and coughed. 'I can't eat any of this bread and cheese tonight. Monro's friend has put me on a diet for my health. I don't think it does much good but I suppose I should give it a chance. What do you think, Jack?'

'I am sincerely sorry you aren't well,' he said, 'but I know nothing about medicine.' He was fingering Tom's sketch and wishing he could take it away and keep it. But the rules were that the host kept the night's productions. He wondered if he could ask Francia to make an exception because it was Tom's last night.

'I wish I could study with you, Tom,' he whispered.

Tom blushed, his sallow skin reddening. 'I tell you what, Jack, I'm going to Paris partly for my health, and partly to do sketches for a possible panorama there along the lines of my Eidometropolis. But when I get back I will give you lessons and I won't charge you. In the meantime you can probably get Monro to lend you some of my sketches he has, if you really want to study my style.

'I doubt if he'll let anything past his front door. I think deep down he is really a selfish person who wants to keep yours and Turner's stuff as an investment. He can be kind and I have to admit he has been good to me, but he has a nasty manner with him sometimes. He hates it if I praise Norwich at the expense of London.'

'Turner's certainly will be an investment the way he is going, but I think you malign the Doctor. Part of him really does want to help, I'm sure. He is probably keen to praise London merely because it is where he lives. He has not seen Norwich. I know myself that he hates the idea of going out of England and his knowledge of it only stretches as far as his place in Surrey, apart from the city itself!'

Cotman turned the subject. 'Did you hear the rumour that Sarah Danby has a child by Will Turner? This will be her fifth, 'cos she already had four by her husband. Will he marry her, do you think?'

'I know he won't,' Girtin said, shifting uneasily because the other Brothers were talking art on the other side of the fireplace and he didn't really want to be out of their conversation and talking gossip with Cotman instead. 'He told me once that he never wanted to clutter his life up with women and children. I expect he will give them something financially and move on.'

'Give them money? I thought he was as mean as the devil. Did you hear how he and his father have put his mother into Bedlam? It's scandalous when he is making all that money. I heard that Monro offered to have her in Brooke House if they paid.'

'Are you talking of Turner?' Underwood exclaimed. 'I heard you mention his mother. Yes, he is a swine to treat

56

his mother like that, whatever she is like. They just live on filthy straw in there and get given emetics to vomit and crap. Everyone says he and his father are monsters, but everyone praises his art and with good reason. He has tremendous talent, though I don't like everything he turns out.'

'Take heed and start working in oils, lads,' Tom said and began to cough again.

'Or better still curry favour with as many influential people at the Academy you possibly can until you get made an ARA,' Francia added slyly.

'Don't you think he deserves his fame? Look at that *Fishermen at sea*.' This was Ker Porter. 'I never guessed when we were fooling about at the Schools together he could do something like that!'

'I personally don't like it,' Tom Girtin interposed. 'It's too full of made-up drama. He likes his work to be full of rainbows or storm clouds.'

'Yes, it's a pity he doesn't stay with his topographical watercolours. My God, they're good. I saw one the other day, *Llanberis Lake and Dolbadern Castle*. If only he'd stick with that sort and not try to make effects and dramas all the time. It's just so peaceful, so noble.' Cotman stopped, surprised to see the Brothers with their mouths open. It was probably the longest speech he'd made since he'd joined.

Underwood said, 'Show Jack Cotman the picture you call your *White House, Chelsea*, Tom. I know you brought it with you. That really knocks anything Will Turner does into a cocked hat.'

Girtin stood up and took the picture from his portfolio. It showed a stretch of the river in the evening, a low sun was lighting up a small white house, end on to the river, near a windmill. The white was reflected in the water of the Thames while the sky was calm with yellowish clouds near the horizon, the banks a grey-blue. The sky indeed took up

57

most of the composition, giving the whole a wonderfully peaceful air.

'You know,' said Tom, 'I met Will Turner the other day. I had this on me and had the temerity to show it him. He actually said something like, "My God, I would give anything to have painted that picture." That, my friends, was one of the best moments in my life.' He sat down coughing, and it rapidly became obvious he had begun to find breathing difficult.

'Quick, Francia, undo his cravat. Give him air!'

The Brothers scurried about helping their friend; luckily this attack was short but Tom Girtin's pallor was worse than ever at the end of it, as he got up to go.

After he had gone the brothers discussed Tom Girtin. 'He's been overdoing it this year. I do believe he's been sketching in Wales, Northumberland, the Lake District and Yorkshire not to mention Scotland,' Ker Porter said.

'Probably getting in as much as he could before he gets married and has to stay at home with the little wife!' Francia laughed.

Cotman, walking home afterwards, thought about this.

Did Tom Girtin's bride realise how ill he was? Could love cure him? Had he, despite his protestations, married only for money? Why should visiting Paris help him? Certainly the climate was little better than London's by all accounts. Was there a future to be made in panoramas? He knew Monro did not think so, but then Monro's own style was limited to the emulation of Gainsborough's, and perhaps he hoped everyone would follow him. He certainly wouldn't think much of Girtin's Paris idea, almost as bad in the Doctor's book as going off to Italy! He laughed to himself.

Thomas's diary

I feel pleased that I have helped the Varleys. Their background is very poor and I suggested they should leave the outskirts of London in Hoxton and settle in Covent Garden among the artists. They have taken my advice and are now in Charles Street. I suppose the fashionable artists are moving ever westwards, as Reynolds did, but their new place will be handy for my house apart from anything else.

I like John particularly. Perhaps he has more talent than Jack Cotman; he is certainly more biddable. If I suggest a change in something he is sketching he does it, not bridling and getting upset as Cotman did the one time I tried it with him. Varley's a great bull of a man, but such a generous soul. I think he needs someone to mind him or he'll be put upon by the unscrupulous. He lost his father young – well, they all did, there's a sister too who has married an artist whom I don't know, by the name of Mulready. John told me wryly once that his father taught him limning and drawing were a bad trade, but perhaps luckily in one way he died when John was but 13 and after that his mother really encouraged him and Cornelius, maybe even Elizabeth too. Apparently Elizabeth corrects her husband's paintings when he is not looking!

John Varley and I went to Polesdon from Fetcham one day to sketch and I particularly liked what Varley did there. He is a pleasant man to have at Fetcham and even Hannah broke her own rule and welcomed him, though she is less happy to see Cotman. Fetcham is big enough as a house for her to be able to keep away from my young artists, but she does come upon them in the garden at times and can hardly with politeness ignore them. Varley is older than Jack Cotman who came to me even younger than my first two lads did, therefore he is more sensible in many ways. He

59

has painted a lot in Wales which has improved his work much, from what I see of his earlier portfolio.

I heard today that Tom Girtin married his goldsmith's daughter. May the gold come his way before the inevitable happens, as I see it. I gather he plans to visit Paris and I fear this is not wise either for his health or his career. He is still keen on these panoramas, but will anyone want to see one of Paris? What it's like living there now just after the Revolution is anyone's guess. I wouldn't fancy it myself. They say he has always had a weak spot for the Jacobins, although that is all over, I suppose. This Peace they've signed: will it hold, I wonder?

At the moment I gather Tom is up in Yorkshire with Lascelles again. Lascelles wrote to me mentioning some wonderful watercolours that Girtin has done for him up there. What a waste of a talent, if what I fear will happen in a year or so, does happen. I can't think he can last long. He came again to plead with me to help him not so long ago. I don't know what to say. Nothing either I nor my colleague suggested has helped him. Perhaps happiness with his wife may lift him a little. We shall see. I am not sure I fully believe that our state of mind can affect our health, though this does seem to be the case occasionally.

Our own boys have had their share of ill health this year, but thanks to good nursemaids and Hannah's untiring solicitude and care, they have survived infancy. Sally is six today and is to start the piano at her own request. I hope it may be a great gift which she can enjoy for the rest of her life. She is always so happy and animated when Edridge comes and sings. It would very pleasant to find she had a real musical gift. As for Robert, Hannah very much hopes he will become a pastor like her father. She knows Tom must take on my job at Bethlem, as I took over my father's. I said to her concerning Robert, 'As long as he doesn't become a Methodist enthusiast. More harm is done to people's minds through Methodism than almost anything else in my opinion. We could empty Brooke House and much of Bedlam even, if they didn't exist, putting depressing hellfire thoughts into people's minds, so that they run mad. I can never understand why they are such a popular sect.'

Our Tom has been a great help to me and I am beginning to appreciate him quite as much as I do Henry, who has, I fear, developed quite a rebellious streak. They have all been enjoying Fetcham this year, playing cricket on the lawns and suchlike. At least then they cannot get into mischief.

I am not too sure I am pleased to hear that Hannah is to have another child after such a long break. She would like another girl and it would be pleasant for Sally, but the good Lord will decide. I hope very much it will be the last baby. Five children is enough.

Talking of which, I hear that Will Turner has fathered a child on a widow with four children already by her husband. I fear he won't do the decent thing and marry her, even though he is supposed to like children. They are all girls I believe, even his own. He always was a selfish oaf, though I pray that he may reform before he grows much older. I refrained from telling this news to Hannah, I knew she would be outraged. Ironic that he is a father of five just as I am to be, but with less effort on his part of course!

One could almost have predicted that Tom would marry and Will would not, but Will is not content to marry his muse, Art, and leave women alone. Oh dear me no, he always wanted the best of all worlds.

The other day he came back to speak to me about his mother, and this time she has been admitted to Bethlem. I went along with his and his father's plans for her, though I disapprove and he knows it. But he is sly; he knows I value him as an artist too much to go against what he wants. In any case I fear she will not last long. I enquired from

Haslam whether Turner or his father ever visit her, but he says they do not. Poor woman, she is impossible. I have interviewed her myself, if you can call it that; she spat and swore at me and tried to hit me until she was restrained. However, I am not related to her and they are. I never cease to wonder where the sensitivity that shows in much of Turner's work can come from when he is totally crass with people and horrible to his nearest and dearest. I hope Mrs Danby gets some affection from him. I wonder if he will provide at least for his own daughter. He is no gentleman, of course, but he is not even one of nature's gentlemen as Varley and Girtin could be called.

The latest inmate we have at Bethlem has given us all pause. He is the famous Hadfield, the man who shot to kill King George at the theatre in May. Apparently he was only a foot away from hitting the King, but the bullet lodged in the ceiling of the royal box, and the King, who must be really quite a brave man, went on bowing to the audience even after the shot was fired. Hadfield was brought to trial but the trial was stopped when he was declared insane. I do not really know if he counts as mad. I suppose a regicide must be insane, but then it depends on the King too. The King has shown clemency already to his would-be assassins; he even asked for Margaret Nicholson, who tried to stab him and who is in Bethlem still, to be looked after. At first she was kept very close, chained, but now she has the free run of the place and is a nice old soul, though it is odd to say that I suppose when you consider what she tried to do. It is amazing that the King has been nearly killed twice. What is it about him that make people want to get rid of him?

The irony of the whole thing is that the King went mad himself two years later. Is it catching? If I was not so interested in art and artists I might get as interested in madness as Haslam is. He says it must stem from the brain

62

and that we ought to study the brain if we want to know more. Haslam told me the other day, at the end of my visit, that Hadfield had been a soldier and sustained a head injury in 1793 in the wars that affected his brain. He tried to kill his son, it appears, and then he met a man called Truelock who persuaded him that if he didn't kill the King the Messiah would not arrive. 'Surely it is Truelock, not Hadfield, who is mad,' Haslam said.

'Well,' I told him, picking up my papers and wishing I could be at home instead of in that draughty, smelly place, 'we can't have murderers running all over the place and if Newgate won't have him, we'll have to, missing brain or no!'

Hannah interrupted me as I wrote this, coming in crying this morning. I had to sit her on my knee and calm her down. She has much nausea this pregnancy and I do feel for her, but I dislike being interrupted. She found me in my study, prior to my first visit of the week to Bethlem. At first I had to listen to her domestic woes and then she was sweet enough to listen to mine. At least, I told her, in the winter months they are not given emetics to make them defecate and vomit. The place smells less, but of course it is colder and the huge cracks in the old building do not help, though I notice Haslam always has a good fire burning in his office. You can't blame him, I suppose. I would not want his job.

I was feeling a little put out on another matter. I had decided, after some thought, that I would no longer visit Turner senior for a haircut. It galled me too much, especially on days when I might already have caught sight of his poor suffering wife during my Bethlem visit. However, I heard through another customer of his that he has given up the barber's shop to spend the rest of his life assisting in his son's illustrious career. I gather he is living with William's mistress and the family while William keeps himself aloof in Harley Street. It made my blood boil.

Hannah doesn't help, either. When she isn't having the vapours she tends to be angry with me. A few nights ago, Cotman brought round Sandby Munn, Francia and Underwood from the Brothers, and the two Varley boys were there too. I had spent several hours in their company and the sketches the Varleys, Cotman and I had done together were held up for inspection and comment. I noticed the lads, as I persist in calling them, were a little reticent when it came to talking about my sketch of trees on a bank with a cottage in the distance. They are probably afraid of my reaction to criticism. I must try and hold my tongue when we are together like this, and not pull rank. It was not one of my best, but on the other hand I didn't think it was at all bad. Afterwards John Varley picked out an earlier one I had done, a gate to a house among trees, and lauded it to the skies. I think he was trying to make amends.

Hannah was angry because she felt I put them before my own boys; something she has said before, but never with such anger and sadness.

'I'm not well enough at the moment, my dear,' I said, 'to give as much attention as I should to the older children.'

She looked surprised that I had mentioned my health, but she said, 'That's all very well, if it is true, but they need their father and yet you persist in playing the father to these teenagers and young men who aren't even of your class!'

'What would you have me do, my dear?' I said.

'Have a talk to Tom. I think it is time he knew more about the family and what part he is to play in the Monro line.'

She was drying her eyes now she saw that I was ready to take my responsibilities seriously, but though I am sorry for her, especially as this later pregnancy was a shock to her, I sometimes feel her emotion is just plain jealousy. I am not sure she even likes me having friends such as Edridge and Hearne, but she cannot attack them so easily. With the lads she can comment on their low-class status and their coarseness. She can compare them with our own children because some are no more than six years older than our Tom.

It galls me that she doesn't want me to have interests and a life of my own. Anyway, as I had promised I had a talk with Tom that evening in my study and asked him what he knew about the Monro family.

'I know we are Scottish and related to a baronet. I know my great-great-grandfather left Edinburgh because he wouldn't swear allegiance to George the First but that it doesn't make us Jacobins. I know that your father and grandfather were both Principal Physicians to Bethlem hospital and that I shall be one day too . . .' He fizzled out, I suppose because he thought it tactless to remind me that I too would grow old and die.

'Yes, Tom, that will be your job, God willing, if, that is, you wish to train as a doctor. It is a long, hard training but I think it is worth it. You probably didn't know that I had a brother John who died before he could inherit it from my father. I then wrote and asked my father if I could be the next doctor and Physician to Bethlem in the family, though I was not the next eldest son. He agreed to it, probably because we both had an interest in art and therefore I was his favourite, but you should really be the one to become a doctor in this family because you are the oldest.

'Your brother Henry I don't think is interested in medicine, but in art. However, we shall see. Practising art, except as an amateur, is not really open to people of our sort as a career.'

This was really too difficult for poor Tom to understand, but he must have told his brother something of it, because Henry came to me crying that Tom said Papa says I cannot be an artist like he is!

*

65

Haslam is in his office at Bethlem, his feet up in front of the fire. It is a foul foggy day and he had felt cold to the bone earlier inside the main building. There is a knock on his door and he just has time to swing his feet down from the fender and turn to his papers, before Dr Monro walks in.

Haslam knows from the way the visitor looks at him, harrumphs and positions himself right in front of the flames, that Monro is not deceived. He had actually been taking forty winks but he had the papers Monro wanted to see in front of him and by quick-wittedness is able to say something relevant, despite some remaining fogginess in the head.

Monro looks down his nose and starts to ask about the chaining of certain individuals and suggests as usual that they should put more opium in their drinks to make them less violent. Then they wouldn't need chains. His point is that several of them got chafed by the chains. Haslam has the air of someone who knows this is the commencement of their usual argument about treatment.

He always points out that he, being resident, is in charge of day-to-day management; that he know the inmates better than Monro does; that there is a shortage of servants and an extreme shortage of reliable ones. Then Monro shifts his stance and counters that Haslam should make more of that to the committee, and Haslam invariably replies that they always respond that they cannot find anyone honest who wants to do the job. The committee will no doubt finally agree to try again to find better staff, and so it goes on.

If only Monro didn't stick his neck into my business, thinks Haslam, feeling the chill of the large figure which cuts out the fire from him, I could run this place a thousand times better, but I have to be under his management, such as it is. I curse myself that he is better qualified than I am. Vomiting and purging the inmates is such idiocy, but because his forebears did it, it might be writ in Holy Scripture as far as he goes.

Once Monro leaves, Haslam warms himself and relaxes a little; he starts to wonder whether to apply for a job somewhere else. At least it might be warmer. But perhaps it is better to put up with the devil you know rather than the devil you don't. At least Monro doesn't come all that often, or merely pokes his head round the door and asks if there is anything special for him to do. All Haslam has to do then is to give him a list, and one of the warders brings the inmates who are sick down to his office and that is the end of it for another day.

The only news that Monro slipped in before he left was that they are getting nearer to finding a new site for the hospital, but of course the committee moves agonisingly slowly, both men know that, and Haslam doesn't believe he will get much relief from this ghastly old building for several years. Nor is there much hope that Monro will give up the job of Head Physician just yet and let his son take over, as he has intimated he will do one day.

'Whoever heard of a dynasty of madhouse physicians? But that is more or less what happens at Bethlem,' Haslam says aloud, as he knocks his pipe out over the fire. 'And they are proud of the fact that they never change anything if they can help it. Well, that's not entirely fair. Monro has managed to get a well installed, I have to give him that.'

Haslam is well aware that he is jealous of the older man, who has a grand house at the Adelphi and a country place, while Haslam must live in Bethlem's cracked and decaying property. He wishes the world of art which Monro loves so much would claim him completely. Surely most physicians don't stuff art down your throat as well as everything else.

As Haslam shrugs himself into his work coat and prepares to go back into the madhouse he looks up at what he thinks

67

of as Monro's pathetic sketches which he does on his travels. It used to be a shared office and Monro, on quitting it, had generously given them to Haslam. The latter is inclined in his present mood to rip them down, but doesn't relish explaining their absence when Monro next calls.

1801

Thomas's diary

When the baby came I was relieved, for Hannah this time was much better than she had been during her pregnancy. 'We will call it John,' I said and added quickly, 'after my father.' To prevent her saying, 'Not after your two young men Cotman and Varley I hope!'

Luckily she likes the name, and Jack he became. I hope now that this is the end of our family. Five children is plenty. Hannah was a little disappointed it was not a sister for Sally, and Sally herself wept on being told she had another brother, but they both cheered up soon after and declared the baby gorgeous.

I hope this new birth is a good augury for the new century. Certainly the news from France is dire and we have had a bad last ten years, with galloping inflation in food prices and fear of invasion from France. The only satisfaction I have, which is no credit to me, is that William Turner has not been able to go to his beloved Italy because no one can get through France.

His trouble, as Hannah has always maintained, is that he's got a huge chip on his shoulder about being common. It is as if he doesn't realise that the better clothes aren't quite enough to change the opinion of the *haute monde*. Beaumont still can't stand him, and maintains his art is bad. All nonsense of course. But Beaumont can't bear the idea that such a poor figure of a man is capable of such nobility and sensitivity in his painting. And indeed it is a wonder to

69

us all where he dredges it up from. He continues to sell his work; people still put up with him and he is even taken into great houses like Petworth by Lord Egremont. (Of course Egremont himself behaves very curiously for a titled man; they say he has as many bastards as servants!)

But I, too, am hypocritical; I, who inveigh against Turner's behaviour, still show off his album, just as I show off Gainsborough's camera obscura. How I remember when Tom and William used to gawp when I first showed them the great man's device.

I am hoping to buy a collection of Gainsboroughs at the sale of his works that his sister is getting up this year. I have been keeping a fund for many years for just this eventuality, although I know Hannah will say we can't afford it, and what about little Jack's education. I suppose I can say it is to celebrate Jack's birth.

Tom Girtin has shown an oil, *Bolton Abbey*, at the Academy, in an attempt to get himself made an ARA. It has had a good press and I am very pleased for him and impressed that he can do all this when he is so often ill. He is at the same time pursuing the idea of a portfolio of 20 Paris drawings, and has finally got the chance to dash over to France now the peace is declared. He wants very much to see the French collections too. Indeed, it occurs to me his energy is a trifle frenetic.

I hear he has had a child, a boy also named Thomas. He was away for its birth. I was glad he had a child, maybe to inherit his talents, but also worried as no woman wants to be left a widow with a child to support if the worst happens. I wonder if Will Turner is jealous that his old friend Tom Girtin had a boy whereas he has had a girl in a family full of stepdaughters, if you can label them so.

It seems a year for babies. Hannah is full of the gossip about Nelson's paramour, Lady Hamilton. They say she has given birth to Nelson's child, though many other reports

70

deny it. She is, after all, still with Lord Hamilton and would *he* not have objected? 'They say she is very fat, so maybe he did not notice,' Hannah suggested, and giggled. 'In any case he is an old man now.'

'I hope you don't follow suit when I am old,' I said to her, and she laughed again.

'Look, it says Nelson has had to return to his ship, but that he and his wife are no longer together, even when he was on land. I feel for her, poor soul,' and she passed me the newspaper.

I shrugged and handed it back. 'It doesn't seem to have ruined his reputation, all this gossip. He is still hero of the hour. His personal life is his own affair, just as long as he is good at fighting off Boney's forces at sea.'

Personally, I don't think she can have given birth, as I heard the gossip from Farington, who had met Benjamin West. He had been at that crazy folly, Fonthill, with Beckford at Christmas and the trio of Nelson, Sir William and Lady Hamilton had also been invited. He was very excited to meet them after all the talk in the newspapers. Nelson is apparently diminutive, almost blind, with of course only one arm. 'What a catch for Lady H,' West apparently said to Farington. As for Emma Hamilton, she was in full fig, West reported, doing some of her peculiar Attitudes, which are based on classical myths and legends. This time, West said, it was more of a play, based on the story of Agrippina. I can't believe she would have done such a thing, heavy with child as she would have been. West saw nothing to make him suspect her to be with child. Of course, he said, she was wrapped up in lots of shawls, but still.

*

John Varley, his elder brother Cornelius and Jack Cotman, are staying at Monro's house in Fetcham; albeit in the attics near the servants and not in the grand first-floor rooms.

There are so many children and servants, the Doctor has less room than the three lads first imagined when the house came into view, and they did not mind that they were all sleeping together in one large bed.

Wednesday is a beautiful day. A marvellous blue day. The Doctor comes striding into the hall where everyone is assembling their equipment, carrying a great hamper which holds lunch.

'Who says England isn't the finest place in the world to live in?' he calls out, and then suggests they walk to a nearby hill and sketch from there. He goes up the hill in the front, gesticulating at the beauties around them and commenting on the fact that Will Turner always wants to go to Italy, 'When he has a place like this on his doorstep, as it were!'

They all nod sagely in agreement that he is mad, partly because it would be hard to beat what they see before them, the meadows rich with flowers, the birds singing, a cuckoo in the distance – and partly because they want to keep their host happy.

Cotman, not wishing to get his shoes muddy, avoids a lane which is half stream after rain the day before, and enters a field, where a bull spies him and starts to give chase. Luckily Varley shouts to him to jump up into the lower branches of an oak tree which grows at the edge of the field nearest the lane. This he manages to do, scrambling up rather clumsily, scratching himself on the sharp twigs.

'What am I to do? I'm sure the great beast of an animal will wait until I'm obliged to come down and then have his way with me,' he yells to the party on the other side of the thick hedge, but the Doctor calms him.

'If you are quiet the bull will get bored and move away. Then you only have to scramble round the back of the tree and through this small gap. We will help you, but don't get stung on the nettles!' Cornelius and John are laughing so

72

much they do not know if they could help anyone, but everyone shouts encouragement.

Cotman does as he is told and ten minutes later he is able to squeeze himself through the undergrowth, getting mightily scratched and stung for his pains.

'A good thing it wasn't John here,' he says. 'He would certainly never have squeezed through that hole!'

Varley looks down at his great girth. It was true, but not very kind, what Cotman had said.

At last they gain the summit and the Doctor suggests they all choose their own composition. Cotman irritates Monro by insisting on walking down the other side to find a little broken fence near a streamlet. Monro himself uses a semi-derelict cottage and a pond for his foreground and Cornelius and John decide on a more general view with gorse bushes in the front of a tree-lined bank.

'Try and improve on that one you did last year at Polesdon, John,' the doctor says heartily. 'I wager you won't be able to.'

Some time later Monro walks down to where Cotman is putting away his equipment and calls to the brothers to come down to a perfect picnic spot in the shade of a great beech. He then distributes a large luncheon, which John particularly indulges in, to the amusement of the others. Everyone enjoys the wine, which slips so easily down their throats, and makes them all sleepy. The Doctor dozes in the sun.

On the way home Cornelius and the Doctor rag each other about their efforts, but then a more serious discussion ensues about whether one should always draw from nature, if it is indeed the best way forward for watercolourists. Here they are all in agreement and Cotman, who has been rather silent since the bull episode, holds centre stage and starts to talk of Girtin and the way Tom's style and choice of subject matter influence his own.

The Doctor seems in no hurry to get home and when they reach the top of the hill overlooking his house, he tells them all to lie down on their backs and listen to the skylarks, which are singing their hearts out above the village. It is hard to forget that moment, even though John Varley can't resist tickling Cornelius after a while and then they all start to roughhouse with each other, even the dignified Doctor! There is a smile on his face never seen in London, and it does not wear off even that evening when they all work up their pictures and then proceed to criticise each other's. The elder Varley tends to be very flattering about the cottage and the trees which Monro has transferred onto a sheet with Indian ink and wash. The Doctor sees through it, but is flattered nonetheless. He says of John Varley's that he will go a long way and be rich, if he does not give away half the money first. Cornelius is shy to show his, mumbling that it is not finished. Jack Cotman is unconcerned, but no one quite knows what to say when he shows them what he has done. They privately think his style too flat and his choice of a broken gate rather odd.

Lying in the bed that night, John Varley thinks what an unlikely foursome they have been that day, behaving like schoolboys, rolling around in the grass and the butterflies, their sketch book pages beginning to blow away in the wind above the hill. He remembers Cornelius running to catch some of his sketches as they nearly fell in a cow pat. Then how Cotman had pretended to push him into it. It had been a particularly large and squidgy one too. He guffaws to himself in an undertone so as not to wake the other two.

He recalls how the Doctor said, beaming, 'This beats any form of doctoring to the mad!'

And how they all ran down the last part of the journey and arrived breathless in his garden. The gardener gave the group an odd look as they sat down on the rustic bench and the Doctor sent off a servant to get them all a drink of small beer. He had taken off his coat for the heat and his hair, usually so neat, was sticking up on end. None of us, Varley thought, looked too marvellous in fact, being covered in bits of dried grass, and Cotman still rather scratched and bloody from the bull episode.

It was sad when the Doctor was handed a note that he had to attend on some patient and, groaning, he went in to change and had his horse brought round, prior to riding off. At least he was able to come back later to join in the tidying up of their efforts, excusing his wife, whom he said had a headache. No one believed him. They knew she always avoided them in London too, though sometimes they saw the children.

As the others snored beside him, Varley lay and wondered if Monro would have trained as an artist had he not been born as a gentleman and thus been forced to train as a mad doctor. He might have been a happier man had he indulged himself in that way, but then, Varley thought, as he lay and looked up at the full moon outside the open window, he would not have been able to afford this house, so perhaps things are better as they are.

1802

Thomas's diary

November. Girtin died yesterday. I put off writing my diary hoping for better news of him as the autumn wore on, but I think we both knew it was hopeless. In fact 1802 has been a sad year in almost every respect, although we must exempt the birth of our little Alexander from this description. Bearing six children has quite spoilt Hannah's figure and affected her energy, but the little boy is the sweetest of all the babes and I named him after my famous great-grand-father. This must be the end, however. Hannah is ageing fast. She feels it sadly, too, that there is only one girl out of the six to keep her company.

I myself have not been well at all this year with an anguish complaint which has sapped my energy. Sometimes I found it hard to mount my horse of a morning and very often had to use my carriage, or the whisky as we call it, to go on my rounds. I dislike doing this, partly as the coachman is always there if I want to stop and draw, and I feel inhibited.

As for Tom Girtin, he came to me a few months ago and pleaded for me to do anything with him just so long as I could put him in the way of carrying on drawing. But there was nothing I could do. He saw it in my face.

His Paris panorama was barely begun and I hear that Demaria has plans to show a Paris panorama along with Hayward, the man who had helped Tom Girtin originally. That must have dispirited him, to be pipped at the post like that by his old collaborator. The Eidometropolis did receive some good reviews. I took Hannah to see it at Spring Gardens. We came up the steps in a darkened room and at the top the panorama suddenly faced us. It was a pleasure to behold, even though I do not like the whole genre of panoramas. So much sensitivity coupled with accuracy. There is a great calm in it, was Hannah's comment when she had got over its size. ('*The Times* says it's 1,944 square foot,' she said, 'and it is so high!') Really, she does have a telling phrase at times. His work *is* very calm. I can only hope that the money they make from the entrance tickets will help the mother and baby, though I presume her father will make over some money to her.

In Hannah's case I shrink from seeing her get out her own paints to start on her execrable flower paintings, about which I school myself to say nice things when they are finished. She knows the truth of what I feel, I am sure. We have not been married 15 years without knowing a good deal about each other's facial expressions! But we keep up this charade, just as many married couples do, I suspect. I don't usually show her my own efforts, but she is always nice about them, too. I wonder what she really thinks.

We actually met Turner at the show and he was very affable (for him). He seemed genuinely cast down about Tom's death, so there is some goodness in him. He praised his work and talked about his promise. 'If he'd lived he would have eclipsed me,' he said simply. 'Have you seen his *White House, Chelsea?*

I said I had not had that pleasure.

'I did not see you at the funeral,' he said next, giving me a sharp look. 'Hearne and Edridge were there, and Beaumont. Many rich and well-connected people came or sent their carriage. He would have been pleased at such a send-off. I was glad I got back from France and Switzerland in time. I had to go and see those mountains, taking advantage of the Peace. You have not been abroad yourself this year, sir?' There was a twinkle in his eye.

'No. I have been ill, and unfortunately particularly unwell at the time of the funeral,' I said curtly, not liking to be upbraided by one such as him, nor teased about my English taste in staying here and painting English scenes only.

'You know he had a child?'

'Yes. I presume the wife is well looked after in terms of money. What a sad and brief marriage that was.'

'She will sell off his work, I suppose, and her father is rich. Poor Tom! We were friends to the last,' he said, and left me abruptly.

I doubted that; there have been many reports of sides being taken in the Academy; those supporting Turner and those who favoured Girtin. Farington never stops telling us the gossip.

He has been to my bedside much this year and with the names of Girtin and Turner on his lips. How Lady Sutherland and Lascelles favour Girtin: they say he has genius and Turner only gets where he does by industry. Beaumont, of course, agrees with them. And so on, and so on.

But to return to the conversation with Will Turner, I hope Tom and Will did keep up. I went home from Spring Gardens and looked over the sketches and copies they had both made in my house. The last time is about five years ago already. I cried a little, which I put down to my weak state of health. I was a little ashamed, as Hannah did not cry when she heard he was dead and I imagined she might have, or perhaps she did in the privacy of her own sitting room. She mostly keeps her tears for her own family.

I heard soon after that Turner had in fact succeeded in becoming a full member of the Academy, not ARA, but full RA. Of course in a way I am not surprised, he has talent and he has courted enough people and Beaumont would say even *bribed* them with gifts of watercolours from time to time. Perhaps that is true. Farington seemed to think it wasn't a bribe when he accepted one.

Farington is a good-looking and energetic man, a sound man where money is concerned too; but he annoys me. Perhaps it is that he is from a family of gentry and yet became an artist and not just an amateur like Sir George. He has broken through a barrier which I believe should never be pierced.

Poor man, he isn't really the same since his wife died. I feel for him, even though he is as irritating as ever. He told me that the King doesn't favour Turner in the Academy because he thinks that Turner's going to France during the peace means he's a revolutionary!

He also told me an amusing tale about Bourgeois, one of the Academy members who favours the King. Apparently he called Turner a little reptile. Of course Will Turner does not like to be reminded of his size and he replied that Bourgeois was a great reptile with ill manners! Well, I said to Farington, the pot really is calling the kettle black now!

I see that the newspapers are usually on Beaumont's side about Turner's latest works. They criticise him for his affectation and absurdity and say that the sea in one picture looks like soap and chalk! Beaumont's version was that Turner's sea was like veins in a marble slab. Turner *is* using too much white in my humble opinion, but I still see him as the greatest genius I am ever likely to have had influence with.

Only one, or perhaps two, good things I have achieved this year. Cotman met the Cholmondeleys through my friend Englefield and Mrs Cholmondeley has asked him to paint up with them at Brandsbury Hall in Yorkshire. He was so pleased to get that chance; he was a different lad when he told me, from the awkward self-deprecating person he used to be. Twenty is a good age to get your break in life and I hope it will be as good as Girtin's was with

Lascelles, though there is less money this time. But they will, with any luck, introduce him to other people of taste and I predict a good future for him, even though like Girtin he will not try anything but watercolour. I hope fervently that his awkward character traits won't resurface and hold him back. He adulates Girtin and was excessively pleased when I one day gave him one of Girtin's copies of Cozens.

Cotman, it seems, has taken over the running of the Brothers now Girtin is gone, and Varley has joined them too. I think Lascelles is to take up Varley now, which gives me much pleasure. I flatter myself I had a hand in that decision.

There was a time when I felt Varley had ignored my advice, especially when he moved to the Oxford Street area and took on those Schutz sisters as pupils, but he still comes to see me and works away at his figure drawing which he knows is his weakness. I can't help him much on that score, not being good at them myself! He teased me in fact about the method I use, sticking on a figure after the sketch is finished. I countered that at least I draw it myself!

They all clamour to see my Girtins now he is dead. They still talk of Will Turner, but it is rather like looking up at a star quite out of their orbit. They do not even try to emulate him.

I think now that I have such a network of young artist friends and acquaintances, there will always be more people to replace the older ones as they move on. I sincerely hope so; I have a taste for their company and I suppose a lust to influence young artists, if only a little. I sometimes cannot resist giving them advice about what to change in their sketches. My portfolios also bulge and my walls are thick with their drawings. Sometimes my biggest fear is fire! I have taken some precautions on that head, in fact, quite recently.

Unfortunately Bethlem tends to take up any spare time I

might have. This year the Governors have had a whole 47-page booklet of rules drawn up, in yet another attempt to get the staff to obey them. We shall meet as a governing body more regularly in future too, except in January, July and August. I suppose the Governors like to have their Christmas and summer holidays too; and that suits me all right while I am out in Fetcham.

I could not help smiling to myself at an occurrence of the other day which all the rules in the world didn't help to stop. Hadfield, the would-be regicide, escaped! There was hell to pay when they found him gone and everyone is keeping very mum about how he managed it. Luckily he was stopped at Dover before he managed to get abroad, where he could so easily have disappeared. Now he is in Newgate, which seems a better place to keep him than Bethlem. I can't help thinking Haslam's laxness is the key to it, but of course he looked wide-eyed innocence throughout the investigation by the governors.

*

Thomas and Hannah Monro are standing in her boudoir, where her new fashionable Egyptian patterned wallpaper of sphinxes and pyramids gazes down upon them.

Hannah is pouring tea from a new Egyptian-style teapot which Thomas gave her only yesterday, but this does not soften her mood today.

'You must not let Sally play so long at the piano, Thomas. She has been this while with me crying her eyes out because her fingers are aching so.'

'She is just playing us off against each other. She knows I wish her to practise now I have bought her the instrument. She also knows you will sympathise with her slightest little pain.'

'She is only just eight, Thomas, what does she know of playing anyone off against each other?'

81

'You'd be surprised.'

'You know nothing about her, except as someone you want to show off to people like Hearne and Edridge. I know her as a person. She's all the companionship I have, in fact.'

'Now you are being ridiculous – you have six children and a husband.'

'My husband seems more interested in talking to his friends than to me! Look at you now, you aren't even sitting down to take tea with me, as I asked, but just standing there arguing and going all red in the face. I do get lonely sometimes; the boys are not much companionship for me, and the babies still in the nursery.'

Thomas sits down rather awkwardly and passes his cup to be filled, then gets out his watch to consult the time.

Hannah, slightly mollified says, 'I know I'm very lucky to have a fine family, all healthy and you providing for us; two houses to live in, but . . .'

'Yes, there is always a but.' Thomas has already rung for his horse to be made ready and is fidgety. He wants to avert Hannah starting on his art protégés and how he prefers them to his own flesh and blood, so he suggests they have an outing together to cheer her up. 'I know you have been much at home with the last baby, but now he is no longer so much in need of you, why should we not attend the play?'

'You know I hate to go out and show my squint, which grows worse. No, don't try to deny it, I look in my mirror and I know what it does.'

Thomas has to content himself with, 'It looks worse to you than to anyone else, I assure you.' He knows she will not go with him to a public event, but it is worth repeating the invitation from time to time. He leaves the house feeling depressed about his marriage.

1805

Thomas Monro has invited his friend Edridge to Fetcham
to draw. They have been out all afternoon and are now
riding slowly home, both weary but fairly contented with
their sketches. Despite it being early November, the day is
not cold and some trees still keep their leaves.

Edridge is expatiating on the great victory of Trafalgar,
which caused all the village bells to ring out that morning.
'This may be the end of Bonaparte, you wait and see,'
Edridge says, turning round in his saddle.

Monro is less sure. 'One sea battle, and Nelson now dead.
I can't see it.'

'Come on! You have been gloomy all day, Monro. What
ails you?'

'It's bad news. I've decided I must give up renting this
house. That's partly why I stayed on here longer this year,
especially with the good weather. But the boys' school fees
cost me more than I care to tell you.'

'I'm most sorry to hear it, but maybe you will be able to
find something smaller, and thus carry on with sketching
and inviting your friends and your "lads" too. Have you
thought of that?'

'I have, but as yet I am unsure what to do. Hannah is not
so upset as I expected. She thinks with my illness earlier
this year I was doing too much. She wants me to get
something nearer her own part of the world; she was born
in Watford, as you perhaps knew. Also she argues it would

not be as far from Watford as from Fetcham to Bethlem and my private homes. No, it's the children who are upset. They love this place and I fear I shall not find a house so pleasant to live in, which is near so many beautiful spots.'

Edridge changes the subject. 'Let's stop and have a glass of something. This dust on the road has made me thirsty, and that inn ahead looks welcoming.'

'The dark will come down if we stay long.' But despite this remark, Thomas has agreed by his looks and they prepare to dismount.

The inn is quiet and they sit in a corner by a window. Edridge asks after the protégés, which he knows will fire up his friend.

'Cotman has been in Wales and John Varley has started his own society. He calls it the Water Colour Society; he doesn't believe in the Jacobin-style of name, The Brothers. You remember Girtin adopted that name although he always said Francia actually thought of it.'

'Yes, I saw that the new society had begun. They say they emulate oil paintings by using gilt frames. John Varley's no fool. I heard that he is doing quite well from its sales.'

'He needs to,' Thomas says. 'He's married a girl with a child already, a fact she kept dark till after the ceremony. But Varley's such a generous soul he probably took it in his stride.'

'I'm glad he's doing well. Don't drink that too quickly; we can't afford to fall off our horses when we try to mount them.'

Thomas grins. 'As for the great Turner, you know he's been calling himself JMW for some time, don't you?'

'I think that was a necessity, there are several William Turners in the art world. He can't afford to be mistaken for a lesser being,' and Edridge laughs his cheerful laugh.

'The M is for Mallord, though the family name as I

happen to know was Mallard, like the duck. Farington says he "lords" it over everyone at the Academy and I won't repeat what Beaumont says. They've been expecting various factions to start quacking when he passes, just to annoy him for putting on airs. There have been several nasty moments with the Hanging Committee apparently; he took Farington's chair which everyone knows is his. I dread to think what Farington said when he came back in the room.'

'I suppose he wants to show he is as good as anyone else. Hasn't that always been his trouble?'

'You're right, and I suspect his mother's dying may have affected him more than we know. You wouldn't think it; they did not even have a burial at St Paul's Covent Garden for her, which was where the couple were married and Will was christened. I know that for a fact.'

Edridge holds his hands out to the fire. 'I heard that he dunned the Marquis of Stafford £20 for a frame when he finished his commission. What a fool he is to make enemies of the powerful and wealthy. I wouldn't be surprised if this new sort of art, all horror and bloodshed, he's been doing won't make him a much less saleable proposition soon.'

'We live in turbulent times, Edridge. I think he's responding to them, or maybe there's something of his mother's madness in him which is finally coming out! You know about his new gallery in Harley Street. He wants to be like Gainsborough and Reynolds, I suspect. Not content just with the Academy to show his stuff.'

'Yes, he always hedges his bets. I admire him for that. He's worldly wise is our Will! He's apparently showing that huge picture he did of *The Deluge*, it's supposed to express the fear we all feel over the war; though I hope no one thinks we will all actually be inundated with water!' And Edridge laughs again, this time so loud the landlord comes out to see all is well.

He offers to have more logs put on the fire, but Monro glances out of the window. 'No, we must go, the dark is coming down and we have a few more miles to ride.'

Both men get up and prepare to go outside to find their horses. 'You know Dayes killed himself,' Edridge says.

'Yes, I heard. He was always odd. I never liked him for the way he consistently put Girtin down. By the way, I don't think I told you that the committee at Bethlem have at last decided to buy a site for the new hospital in Islington. A good airy place. I am so pleased. I think the ghastly old place was helping to put me in hospital myself, though I hope not a mental one! Hannah is sure that is one reason for my latest illness. Well I am forty-six, no longer a young man, eh Edridge!'

'Cheer up, Thomas, you are still in the prime of life.'

'Nonsense, you're thinking of yourself, a mere thirty-six and look at the way you vaulted into the saddle a moment ago.'

Edridge is pleased, because he knows he has cheered his friend, despite what he says of his age. Monro is generous to him and he wishes to do what he can in return. 'I predict you will be having several moves in the next year, not only the hospital but a place near Watford maybe.'

'You are a good friend. Yes, perhaps things are looking up and I should start looking around for a country place on a smaller scale. What do you say to a cosy supper in my study when we get in and then both of us try and perfect our sketches.'

'And if we have time I would like to hear Sally play her latest piece and maybe have a bit of a singsong with me.'

'That first, then a good meal, a good hour or so with our sketches and finally bed.'

1807

Thomas's diary

I am delighted. I have at last rented another country place, this time north of London which pleases Hannah. Merry Hill is in Bushey, a small village quite near Watford. My other reason for trying this area was Edridge having once gone sketching at Bushey Mill with Hearne and Girtin about six years ago. He always said what a perfect unspoilt spot it was and I still have the sketch he made there of Girtin himself sketching, which I pull out when I feel nostalgic. I should have been with them but for some reason I could not go; now I have Edridge's marvellous drawing to help me feel I was there.

It is just a small cottage but I hope we can add to it, if finances allow. Tom is grown now and will come perhaps less often. And Henry is to go to sea. Bob will not be far behind him in spreading his wings, so that will mean only three children left at home. I didn't realise how much I missed Fetcham until I unpacked my goods in Merry Hill and realised I was breathing more peacefully and regularly and my muscles all seemed to relax. I hope and trust we will be merry here.

I have also begun to see a new generation of lads, which Hannah says is why I am so happy again.

Of course we are still at war. It's funny, Turner of all people turned very patriotic and painted several pictures of the battle of Trafalgar. None of them very good in my opinion. Beaumont always said his foregrounds are comparatively blots. Beaumont is in fact getting incandescent on the subject of Turner, who he says is trying to paint like Claude, 'Like the great Claude, what a cheek,' he says. I've heard on the other hand that Turner maintains he was never so relieved as *not* to be taken up by Beaumont who, he says, drops artists like hot potatoes as soon as they don't do exactly as he says.

There is truth in that and certainly everyone I know gets very tired of Sir George pretending to be the arbiter of all artistic taste. However, I know from personal experience that he can be very generous. He genuinely loved Cozens, partly for his father's sake because Sir George was taught by Alexander Cozens as a boy and said he was a really charismatic teacher. Of course Beckford also knew Cozens père but he didn't love the son! Said he was a rascal or some such thing. Beaumont and I both share a love for old Hearne. For Beaumont he was the king of all painters when he was young; he is very fond of telling the story of how he was taken to Hearne's studio as a lad by his tutor.

Certainly Beaumont lives and breathes art, much more than I do in my conversation, but then he lays down the law even to the professionals, which they do not like. He has shown his own amateur productions at the Academy for many years and tends to scoff at watercolours, and especially at Varley's attempt to raise the status of them with his society. When he told me it was rubbish, he obviously didn't remember that my interests lie solely in these things; a lapse which I can't help holding against him. He might be a little more tactful, but then he has all the baronet's air about him, however polite and genuinely democratic he appears at times.

People sometimes compare me with him, when they come to see my collection, but I do not encourage the comparisons. I always demur and say I am nothing to the great man. They can find irony there if they want to.

We couldn't help being amused a few years ago when a moonlight picture he did was rejected as trash by most professionals, and last year some said the tone of his pictures overall was low. Amateurs should not try to be professionals; it only angers both sides, in my opinion.

It is lucky he now has a more important venture on his hands, rebuilding a family pile at Coleorton in Leicestershire. It is nearing completion, with Dance as his architect and even the great poet Wordsworth designing the gardens. What does a poet know about plants, I wonder?

Unfortunately he also has a finger in the pie of this new so-called British Institution; I think this competition with the Academy will not do much for British art, but split the parties concerned. Turner is already fulminating against him, I hear, despite knowing Beaumont can do him harm professionally. Sir George is hoping to get government money to set up a national collection: ambitious ideas, but if you don't think big, you don't get anywhere. I certainly like the idea of a national collection.

Sometimes I do feel a little jealous of Beaumont's leisure, his power and wealth. If I didn't have to spend 90 per cent of my life with the patients, what could I not do? But there you are, I am only descended from a baronet indirectly, I am not a rich man and Sir George has no children, either. Poor man, he and his wife do not know the joys of parenthood, but neither have they had to suffer from the expenditure involved, nor the anxieties.

Talking of which I have had bad news of Cotman, who has been up in Yorkshire with the Cholmondeleys and their friends the Merritts. I thought he was on his way to make his name and perhaps his fortune. He taught Francis Cholmondeley, his mother and his four sisters and apparently they knew him as 'Cotty.' But he came back to London and for some reason I do not understand and Varley is unable to explain, he did not get voted on to the membership of the Water Colour Society. This must have been a double blow, as he was so keen on Girtin's Brothers and was even head of it for a while. I haven't seen him for a year or so, and now I am told he has gone back to Norwich in a pet. It will be much harder for him to make a name for himself there, and how many patrons will he have contact with? I fear his rather difficult personality must be to blame; but Varley did say that his style was disliked by many in the Society, though the Merritts and Cholmondeleys must have liked it as well as his character. Or perhaps there was a cooling off there too. I always remember how Cotman refused to sketch what he was asked to, and sometimes would not copy what I set him to do. A tricky customer at times!

Well, Hannah said that not all my geese would turn into swans and she was right, no doubt. All the same I think there must be factions in this Society and perhaps he crossed some people, who were not part of the original Brothers.

Cristall, whom Varley introduced me to, an older man than my usual protégés, has become ill. They say it is overwork as he has done much with this new Water Colour Society. I was called in and prescribed complete rest. He is gone down to Hastings, paid for by the generosity of Varley and others. I went so far as to waive my fee, and I think Beaumont paid something into the fund. Let us hope he recovers his health there.

Our latest excitement at Merry Hill, not so merry with him about, as Hannah aptly remarked, was a visit from the great JMW! He came to dine with me, Hoppner and Edridge; I could not help wondering if he wanted something from either of them, but perhaps not. He said he wanted to come and see my new country residence and, if he was disappointed with its size after Fetcham, he had the grace not to say so. He has been staying at Cassiobury Park with my aristocratic neighbour. He told us that he had that day, in fact, been trying to finish a picture of reapers in Cassio-bury Park, which he had originally sketched out of doors. 'But my heart is not in it,' he said. 'I shall probably leave it unfinished.'

I had to excuse Hannah who resolutely refused to see him, and ate upstairs, even though I knew she would be peeping from behind the curtains to get a glimpse of him when he arrived. I said she was indisposed but I knew that he realised that was a lie.

I can't say he has got much better at eating in company since the oyster days, but he was at least better dressed and looked reasonably clean. There was touch of condescension in his manner to me, but occasionally the eagerness of the boy shone through and at times I even began to quite like him. I said as little as I usually do in company, but the others almost fawned upon him, which I'm sure he must have enjoyed.

They discussed the new star on the horizon, Wilkie, as yet quite a boy, who took the art world by storm with his *Village politicians* last year. Personally I do not like these genre pictures, but certainly the crowds buzzing round it at its Academy showing suggests it has set a new trend. It reminded me a little of Hogarth's way of depicting people. My father never really got me to like Hogarth, though he had collected some, which I sold when he died. I call these pictures vulgar, but I said nothing and listened to what Turner was saying.

Beaumont, whose name he always says with a sneer, has taken Wilkie up and commissioned a picture from him, called *The blind fiddler*. I have actually seen it and tried to say nice things about it at the time for Beaumont's sake, he was so enthusiastic about his new find. At the same time I happen to know that Wilkie is near nervous exhaustion and that Beaumont offered to send him to Madeira to recover. Turner surely does not know this, though he would hardly bring himself to praise Beaumont for anything he might do, even if he knew it. He said with a chuckle that he had decided to show Wilkie up a little with a genre scene of his own, which he had humorously entitled with the tongue-twister *A country blacksmith disputing upon the price of iron and the price charged to the butcher for shoeing a pony*. Of course he was having a go at the new tax on iron at the same time. So our Will is not without a grim humour at times.

Edridge said he supposed Turner disliked the new lad, but Turner said no, in fact he liked Wilkie who was very amusing and he hoped they would be friends rather than enemies. He said that Wilkie admired his (Turner's) pictures, which of course helps, as far as our JMW goes!

He turned to me and said, 'I had to find out if Beaumont would be here tonight before I considered coming over, as I conclude you still see him.'

'Oh yes,' I said calmly. 'We are old friends, but I would have seen to it that *he* would not meet *you*; never fear.' I hoped he noticed the way I put that.

But Turner merely remarked on the irony of the fact that Beaumont had rubbished his *Goddess of discord*, saying it was the work of an old man. 'And myself not yet thirty-two,' he said smiling. 'The old "aristocrat" admitted I had ideas still but added the caveat that I had lost the ability to express them!'

'I don't think Sir George can do you much harm,' I remarked. I had not meant that to mean I was taking sides, but he seemed gratified.

'He will do his best to destroy me, but I am glad to see you, the good Doctor, do not follow the trend of gossiping against me, as I know Farington does, and others who want to keep in with him. He is a powerful man, no doubt of it. But I have a few tricks up my sleeve. I flatter myself I can turn my hand to any style he can promote to try and show me up.'

We discussed the British Institution, which Turner condemns as run by connoisseurs not artists. Edridge joked about it, but I thought Turner looked glum. He is tremendously ambitious and I have to say very hard working. His father does the dogsbody work of fetching and carrying for him, I believe. In fact he is quite the little wife that Turner never had.

Edridge dared to ask him about his family (there is another girl, Georgiana, now), safely stowed away in the country in Great Missenden. He said little about them, but expatiated on his own move to Hammersmith. 'I have ever loved the river,' he said, 'and now I am with the nobs. Lord Burlington is just down the way and Hogarth's old house is near, for artistic credentials, and among the living de Loutherberg is round the corner, whom Beaumont claims is superior to me of course!'

Hoppner said ingratiatingly that he much preferred Turner's *Shipwreck* to that 'stupid avalanche' of de Loutherberg's. Turner was pleased and thanked him very graciously, I thought. So perhaps he did want something from this evening; the support of some of the old guard in art circles.

Tom and Henry were both at the meal, Henry lapping up all the talk of art, but Tom rather less interested. He likes talking literature and loves Shakespeare, just as my father did. I joke that that ability missed a generation! Henry was too shy to ask Turner anything, but I knew from his face and the way his hands moved that he was itching to do so. He would dearly love to follow the same career path that Turner has done, but I have been firm.

'You cannot as a gentleman's son become an artist,' I say. He always maintains this is not true, and even if it is, then he will be the first to show that up as a lie. 'But,' I say, 'they are only workmen; we as amateurs, as virtuosi, are above them. You must make your career at sea. I have contacts that will help you there.'

He argues and Hannah pleads that we do not send him into danger during this time of war, but I can see that he hasn't the talent that any of my protégés have, although he does have *some*. But I have made up my mind and that is that.

I prefer to think of happier things, and my new set of lads is what I try to keep my mind on, during the long miles of journeying on horseback, when I am with the mad people and certainly when I am with Hannah and Henry.

Linnell, another John, is only 14 or 15, and knows Mulready, Varley's brother-in-law. He, I suspect, may be a little sly, just as Turner was. We shall see, he is young yet. Hunt is a little older and is of particular interest to me because he is a cripple. He is very brave about it and we have devised a way he can sketch, by his being wheeled about in a sort of barrow with a hood if it rains, pulled by our donkey, Nell. There is Munn from the Brothers and De Wint, who is Dutch (he adores Girtin's work and always sits gazing at my pictures by him, trying to emulate him). Though he is 22, I try to act a little as a father to him. His own father has cut him off with a shilling for having a romantic attachment to a Scottish girl. But he is strong and decided to make his own way in life. Shepherd is 24 and has already won the Silver Palette at the Academy two years running, and then there's Reinagle who is only 12 or 13. There is Glover, too, who has a club foot but is so brave, and I do everything to help him to get about. I know myself what it is to have a bad foot. I have even had a friend look at it for him, but there is not much that can be done. I like his work, though I do not know if he can ever make a name

94

for himself. A real mixed bag, and all coming to me through Varley, whose pupils they are. I still pay them, per hour, and the rate has gone up a little since Turner and Girtin's day. They are none of them as good, but I am cognisant that money does not buy so much as it did 12 years ago.

They enjoy coming out to Bushey and seeing my new collection which I have pasted wall to wall in my rooms. I just surround each watercolour or sketch with gilt beading to give the suggestion of a frame, which is much cheaper than buying a wooden frame for each, and I flatter myself looks just as good. Linnell, however, dared to criticise my exhibition method! I do not think I like him but I can see he may be the most talented and the one with the most personality too.

Varley teaches them direct from nature. Although I agree nature is our best teacher (something Sir George would endorse as well), I also think that copying the masters is a worthwhile thing to do and that is why at Adelphi Terrace I still use the practice. So far they do not demur.

I think Hannah was surprised and also rather grumpy about a new influx of lads, but the children welcomed them, especially Henry of course, as he can talk to them about art and they are kind and always try to help him, indeed some of them are his age or thereabouts. One or two of them are a little flirtatious with Sally too, but I am glad to say she keeps her dignity and usually retreats to sit in her mother's boudoir. I hope she is wise enough not to tell her mother the reason! Robert, too, finds them a little tiresome at times. He is more studious than Henry, who has certainly caused some problems with his lack of application at school.

As I watch they are all out playing cricket with the lads in the garden, except poor Hunt, but he is sitting in his cart clapping when someone gets a run or catches someone out.

What a charming boy he is. Even Hannah is drawn to mother him, even though our two youngest are only just out of the nursery themselves.

*

The three eldest sons of Thomas Monro are sitting in Tom's room at Merry Hill house. They have long faces as they can hear their parents' voices rising from the room below in heated discussion. They all know it is because their father invites so many young artists out to Merry Hill. The boys, however, are on his side, as they have had some good times playing cricket with the lads. The day before, they had even got the men who were wallpapering the little study to come and join in when there was a shortage of people to field.

'It's hard on Mother, all the same,' Tom says.

Henry disagrees. 'She's just jealous of Father's interests outside the home. I think having artists around makes our house special.'

'Only because you like art yourself,' Bob says. 'Father's got no time for anyone but you. The only time he is pleased with me is when my report from school comes and it says I have worked hard, but when he reads yours, Tom, and sees how well you've done in the classics and English, I tend to be nowhere again.'

'My report from school was terrible. Well, you know how Father beat me!' Henry says. 'So much for being his favourite. I'll swap you any time, Bob.' Henry is actually trying to sketch both his brothers, which is why they are all assembled in the biggest bedroom. 'Oh, why can't I get a likeness!' Henry rubs out the lines he has just drawn in.

'Hurry up,' Bob says. 'I'm tired of sitting in one position like this.'

'I won't take much longer, and then it's your turn Tom, if you don't mind. There goes Father again, roaring at Mother. In any case, Bob, you're Mother's favourite, apart from Sally of course. She thinks you're going to take over from where Grandfather left off, and be a vicar! Anyhow as the old man is dead set on this idea of sending me to sea, I'm lost. How can I draw at sea or make my way at all?'

Tom laughs, 'Well, you can start by drawing the ugly mugs of the crew and then get inspired by all the tropical islands you visit. We'll expect lots of pictures of palm trees and natives dancing on the sand.'

'Not with a war on. You seem to forget it will probably keep on until I've been shot to pieces in a naval battle.'

This silences the three, until Tom gets out some tarts which the cook has smuggled to him.

'I'm going to run away and become an artist, anyway,' Henry says.

'What will you do for money?' Bob asks, stretching at last, now Henry has started on his sketch of Tom.

Henry mutters he will find a way. 'It is so wrong of Father to encourage all those other lads to become artists, and yet discourage his own children. I'm sick to death of him telling me that gentlemen don't become professionals, they are better off as dilettanti. Yet he always praises my artistic efforts and seems to want me to carry on.'

'He sees you as his former self. That's why. At least I don't have to worry about what I'm going to do. How would you two like it with the Monro Bethlem "succession" hanging over your heads? I know Father realises I'd like to write about Shakespeare, but will he let me? No, I must do my medical training and be a good boy.'

'Oh, it's not such a bad life, Tom. Look how he thrives on all those mad people! At least you won't have Bonaparte's guns firing at you while you're being seasick overboard!'

'I wonder what Sal will do, apart from get married I suppose. It's so much easier for girls,' says Tom.

'Father will make her practise so much her hands will

probably fall off,' Henry says, dropping his pencil and rolling about with mirth suddenly.

'I saw something yesterday, do you think I should tell Mother? One of the lads was trying to kiss our Sal behind a bush in the garden. They ran off when I called out and I wasn't sure which one it was. It can't have been Hunt because he could not have run! Linnell would be too religious, I suppose. Perhaps it was De Wint. I just told Sal I had seen *something* and she blushed and told me not to be a telltale or she would get her own back one day. In the end I promised not to. But I noticed today Sal was up with Mother in her boudoir and did not come down, which she usually does if we are planning a game of cricket.'

'At least don't tell Father, Bob,' Henry says, sobering up. The voices below have stopped.

'I suppose Father finally got his way about the lads coming,' Tom says, preparing to get up. 'Have you nearly finished, Henry? I want to go to bed. Poor Ma!'

'She loves her babies and she's got Sally. I don't think she has a bad life compared with us. At least he doesn't beat her. There! It's finished. Any good?'

'You've got Tom's mouth and eyes very well,' says Bob admiringly. 'It's better than the one you've done of me.'

*

Will Turner is with Sarah in Isleworth, the father now of two strapping girls, Georgiana, now nearly walking, and Evalina, already six. Danby's four noisy offspring complete the household.

Despite the beauty of the river outside, Sarah is overwhelmed with children and too much alone. This morning she is half awake and already telling Will that he does not treat her as a husband should.

'For the very good reason,' he says, dressing himself quickly, as he has things to do, 'that we are not husband

98

and wife. You know very well you will lose your pension from the Musicians if you marry me. We have gone over that enough times in all conscience.'

'We can always marry secretly,' she says, putting down the baby and getting out of bed herself. She smells strongly of sour breast milk on her night-gown and he turns away from her.

'So what would be the point of that if you want to become my wife in the eyes of the world?'

'Who says I do?' she says, taking off her night-dress and exposing her ripe warm body, beginning to grow flabby after so many lyings in, but still desirable enough, even though he is due to travel into the Academy today to see Farington and is already late.

He wrenches himself away from her grip, because she always knows his mood and she has put her arm about him, rather to strangle him than to excite emotion, it feels.

'I have to go. I need Farington's vote to get me the post of Professor of Perspective at the Academy. The vote is soon now. Please, Sarah my love, it will mean more money coming in and I promise to buy you a new gown if I get it. There now,' and he pushes her off as gently but firmly as he can.

'You are too strong,' she said, glowering but still sexually aroused, he can see. 'I don't need gowns, I prefer your company. Why should we have to live so far away from you and put up with the odd gift thrown our way like starving dogs?'

'You exaggerate,' he says. 'I have my career to think of. Count yourself lucky you have a provider when you have so many brats.'

'Two of which you fathered on me! I wish I'd never met you,' and she starts noisily to cry.

So after all it ends as he had not meant it to, with Will down on the bed with her again, unbuttoning his breeches and giving her what she wants. Will is, of course, then late for Farington but luckily he too had been held up, so he does not mind as much as he might have.

Will rides to town, thinking about the problem that is posed by Wilkie's *Village politicians*. It still rankles that his own *Village blacksmith* had been criticised by those stupid critics as not highly finished enough to compete with Wilkie's picture, the latter being so full of those little domestic details, which the crass public at the Exhibition had spent hours examining. Well, he thinks, I shall no longer take account of this stupid new fad in art, but do what I do best. Wilkie himself was kind about my picture, but of course he was probably in secret congratulating himself on how he had bested me at the exhibition, where I had tried to outdo him and failed. I have learned my lesson. I am not interested in genre pictures and I shall not do any more if I can help it.

1808

Henry Monro is on his way home; running away as he is from his ship. He has impulsively knocked on his friend John Constable's door in Cecil Street, not daring to turn up at his own house. John is kind and takes him in, even though he is in the middle of a very big picture and needs to get on with it. He gets him a hot negus.

'So what in the world has been happening to you?'

Henry starts to explain. 'I was so homesick when I got to my ship, even after the kindness of Mr Bates the mate, who tried to make it seem less horrible. I did like him so, he was interested in my art and very grateful when I gave him one of my efforts. He stuck it up in his cabin. But the rest of the crew were so rough and kept telling me all the horrors of sea sickness, then what a battle at sea was like. They really seemed to enjoy telling me all the gory details; surgeons chopping off legs and arms without anything but a swig of rum, if you're lucky, to take the pain away, blood running all over the deck.

'The captain was cold and took very little notice of me and Mr Bates was not always there to help; he had his duties and could not be seen to favour me in front of the men. I never felt so alone, and although I wrote home and bravely said I would be sending them sketches that I did from the ship, I knew then that I would not be able to stand it. I even started to be sick when we were waiting for the

101

right wind, off Yarmouth. They jeered at me and said, "Just wait till we get into the North Sea."

'At last I made a run for it when we had to go ashore for provisions; I was lucky to get a chance. Looking back I don't know where I found the courage or why no one caught me.' He catches hold of Constable's coat sleeve. 'John. I've got to make a career as an artist like you; I know now I could never set foot on a ship again and certainly not with the threat of being killed in a battle hanging over me. I'm a total coward.'

'You're not, Henry. You've merely had the sense to realise you have a gift and you want to use it.'

John advises him, as Henry suspected he would, to go to the Academy schools if he can, and ignore his father. He is very sympathetic because his father, too, had not wanted him to be an artist and it had taken a long time for him to make up his mind to come to London.

'I couldn't stand the work Father wanted me to do, Henry,' he says earnestly.

John Constable comes from East Anglia and many of his pictures are of that region. Henry admires his work; John is passionate about nature. He started himself nine years ago at the Academy schools and rented the house where he now lives at the same time. His father is a rich corn merchant who very much wished that his son would follow in his footsteps and work in the counting house, which he did do, but only for a short time.

He tells the runaway, while they are downing some ale together later, that last year he had gone to the Lake District on the recommendation of his uncle, to paint the wild scenery there, but he says he felt rather overawed by the mountains and the solitude. He prefers an inhabited countryside. This year he has exhibited three pictures, all of the Lake District area, but he longs to paint his native country, even though the prevailing taste seems to be for more romantic, wild spots. He laughs and says his father told him that not so long ago that sort of mountainous scenery was considered downright ugly. 'He, like me, prefers his home county,' John says.

He knows of Monro senior's association with Turner, whom he holds in awe but is not sure that he understands. He says he has seen him at the Academy, where Turner is now a professor, but has never really spoken with him.

Henry finally plucks up courage to go home, armed with the advice that Constable has given him. He knows the interview with his father will be stormy, not to say unbearable. He also knows that Constable is not an artist in his father's set, which means he will be uninterested in what Constable has had to say. He will also maintain that the Constables are not gentry but merely corn merchants who have made a fortune out of it. A very different case to Henry's own family.

Henry hesitates before ringing his own bell. He hopes and yet fears that his father will be out, which he is likely to be in the middle of the day. His mother will be upset and shocked, but at least will side with him.

Monro is in, as it happens, and takes the lad into his own study, looking very red and then very white.

'So I gather you have decided to take the law into your own hands and undo all the good I have done you. Pray, what shall I say to Mr Bates, who has been so kind, let alone to the captain of your ship?'

Henry bravely suggests, 'Tell him I was too much of a coward to face a naval battle.'

Monro is not sure what to say for a moment. 'I suppose you think you are going to take up a paintbrush and make your fortune from now on, is that it?'

'Well, not my fortune, but yes, sir, a living of some kind.'

'Of *some* kind,' he repeats heavily.

Then comes the part about Constable and as predicted

103

the answer that the Monros are a cut above the Constables and so what John Constable suggested does not apply.

'You come from good stock and I am in an eminent position. I have this year been dining frequently with the King's doctor after this latest madness of King George,' Monro states, after mentioning that he is a member of the Royal College of Physicians, and listing all the offices he holds in the curing of the mad.

Henry tells him as a parting shot not to be selfish when thinking of his son's career, which of course brings on his most icy of moods for several days. Thomas does not like the idea of being compared to Constable's father, someone who thwarts a promising artist son, even though that is exactly what he *is* doing.

In the days that follow, Henry keeps out of his father's way as much as possible. His mother tells him that she thinks the Doctor is softening towards the idea of his training at the Academy, once the embarrassment of writing all the letters needed to get him out of the Navy is completed. 'He knows one or two people whose families are not much below ours socially who are sending their sons, so perhaps it will all end well.' She tells him also that she is very relieved to have him back safely in the family and not out in a war-torn naval ship, where she feared for his life every minute of the day.

One day Henry sees his father's protégé Hunt, who comes to the house. Hunt is not much older than Henry and in the past had encouraged him, but now he dare not say too much as the Doctor has been good to him. He is now teaching the daughters of Lord Essex at Cassiobury Park, the Monros' neighbours in Bushey, which is a job which the Doctor procured for him. Hunt can only smile and say he is very glad to see Henry so soon again.

1810

Thomas's diary

I got my friends Hearne and Edridge and Farington together for a long stay at Merry Hill this summer. Hearne is getting old and is really stuck in his ways, but he has long been my friend and I cannot forget that. Edridge is always fun in a group, full of songs and jollity. Sally enjoys his visits as he loves to sing with her at the piano and always pays her compliments. She is a wonderful little musician, he says, and I have secretly to agree with him. He added, rather to my annoyance, however, that he had noticed her hands were slightly out of shape from all her practising. Thank God she did not hear that, nor Hannah, who is always saying I kept the child at it too much.

I know she wishes Edridge would bring his wife, but he never mentions her and I do not like to pry into his matrimonial affairs. He is in fact thinking of renting a place near us here in Bushey. I wish he would succeed in the plan and perhaps Hannah would then see more of his wife.

Farington was as usual full of art world gossip. I wanted to know what they thought of my idea of sending Henry to the RA schools and surprisingly they were all for it, so he has started there and is so much happier and nicer an individual that I have quite forgotten the times when he was rude to me and refused to do what I said. Probably, as Hannah always declares, it was a mistake to send him to sea, but I had the best intentions. I still have reservations as to how he will fare in the art world but, as he points out, several of my protégés have done well, notably Turner and Varley. I forbore to say that some have not; poor Girtin is dead and Cotman is hardly ever heard of now he is in Norwich. What a waste of two talents.

Hearne was very rude about Turner's work. He once said that his skies are the skies of a madman! So Beaumont is not the only one who dislikes him and Hearne still draws superbly. He knows what he is talking about. He has just finished his last volume of *The Antiquities of Great Britain*, which have been coming out for over 30 years.What a legacy to leave behind one! No wonder he has aged, it has been a huge project and he can deservedly rest upon his laurels now.

Farington was full of the RA news that Turner is not fulfilling his duty to lecture in perspective since he has been made professor of it. Perhaps he is afraid to give a lecture, knowing how poorly he expresses himself and with what an accent. One wonders why he was so keen to get that job; status, I suppose. Farington says that the latest gossip is he's taken Danby's niece as his housekeeper, while his mistress, her cousin, is kept in the country with the brats.

If it is just money that is stopping him having them all together in one house, he has plenty of that by now, and like this he must pay for two establishments, instead of one. But I don't think that Turner ever means to marry.

Farington also told us that Turner is getting many of his works engraved for a book he calls the *Liber Studiorum*, on the lines of Claude's *Liber Veritatis*; this is a way of stopping people copying his work. Hearne growled into his soup that Turner had a cheek to compare himself with Claude like that. I agreed, but I did not say so, as it would only be passed on in Farington's gossip to the next person.

Beaumont is getting more and more scathing about Turner, and West too has been quite rude, talking of crude blotches, his version of Turner's latest. One does rather

106

wonder how they managed to vote him in as a professor of perspective, if none of them favour him. After all West is the President of the Academy now.

I sometimes feel for Will Turner. I know how he cares about adverse criticism; it does not pass over him as it does with some. But he will only be more determined to succeed the more he is criticised, that I do know.

After Farington left Henry did some very good imitations of him, though I told the boy he was most rude. I stressed that he had better keep in with Farington if he wishes to do well at the Academy. To do him justice he was somewhat chastened by that thought.

I have to admit Farington is a tiresome person. He wanted to see my pictures that I had recently displayed at Merry Hill and then was rather impolite about how I had hung them. I felt it was really none of his business. He also commented rather unnecessarily about my fatter figure; I certainly need to lose weight but now I cannot walk well or without pain I do not get the exercise I used to. Hannah should not encourage me to eat so much, or else employ a worse cook. I do strive to eat less, but after a long day in the saddle I seem to need sustenance.

One visitor I was interested to meet this year was Henry's friend Constable. He was a little wary of me, I suppose Henry has painted me as a dragon, but we had an interesting exchange of views and of course have many acquaintances in common. I shall take more interest in his work from now on. He is very indebted to Beaumont, he says, who has allowed him to see his Claudes which he venerates. I tried tactfully to hint that Beaumont tends to take people up and then drop them without warning, but he seemed not to notice my remark. Perhaps he will be able to stay in Sir George's good books. He is a much pleasanter and more biddable person than Turner, though someone told me he can have a sharp tongue. Perhaps he has the sense to show

107

only his charming side to Sir George. He strikes me as very ambitious, however.

Probably one has to have ambition to succeed as an artist, though Varley, who is so happy-go-lucky, gets by. I fear that Henry does not have that sort of drive, but perhaps I am wrong. He is young yet.

I have some consolation in doing up and improving my country place. This year I have rooted out several hedges in the fields I have bought around the place and am planting them up as gardens and orchards. Sally thinks I should not get the hedges rooted out as the songbirds will miss them. I tell her I am as fond of songbirds as she is and that there has been no diminution of song since I took the hedges away. They will merely nest in my fruit trees instead.

I have also added on to the house a little which has proved rather more disruptive. I flatter myself it no longer looks so ordinary.

1811

Thomas's diary

This has been a bad year so far, perhaps the worst, even counting 1808 when Henry ran away from his ship, the *Amelia*. I have had a bad illness and I thought little of the doctor who attended me. He was nervous, knowing I was lately become an Elect of the Royal College of Physicians. I did as he said but I am not entirely sure that bloodletting ever cured anyone, except perhaps lunatics.

The wonderful thing was that Henry was most kind to me and was my principal nurse, despite all our struggles of the past years, and I have given him in recompense all my Watteaus, which I know he has long coveted. They are no great loss to me as I am not so much enamoured of that style as I was when I was younger. Henry is always a worry as he still fails to settle. For instance last year he got engaged to his cousin Julia, and he decided he would throw up art and join the army like her brother Frederick, before having a change of heart. He also had an offer from the Culling Smiths to take up a government post. I know they are influential and related to us, but I am still quite pleased he refused them. They irritate me exceedingly when they suggest how much better class they are than us.

He seems to have decided art is his mistress after all, which in some ways I am relieved to hear. I do not want a son who changes his mind about his career every year or so. He started off having a studio at the top of the house and bringing his models there, but Hannah strongly disapproved, thinking the worst about these women, and, thanks to me, he now has a studio in Covent Garden where he works. He managed to show four pictures this year at the Academy, but then gave us all a terrible fright by falling from his horse and wounding himself quite badly. I was really too ill myself to take it in at a serious level, but Hannah was in a terrible state with two of her men, as she put it, very ill at once. She was relieved, however, when he broke off his engagement, as she never liked Julia very much.

Tom is steady; I know, though the family don't think I do, that he has occasionally helped to pay off Henry's debts and I am glad that he is the one who will take on the Bethlem job when I am gone. Bob is very pious and close to his mother, so it is only Henry who creates difficulties. We shall see if the two youngest will react more in Henry's way or like their calmer brothers.

I am getting old and tired; the thought of those boys growing up and making problems is too much for me. All my mad patients, my private ones and my Bethlem ravers, take up my energies when I am well and I cannot do with too much upset at home. Hannah at least is calmer and sweeter than she was, relieved not to be child-bearing now, and there are fewer of my old protégés around these days to vex her, although we still see Hunt and Linnell, and even Varley sometimes.

Hoppner, my old friend who is roughly my age, died last year which gave me much to think of. I am only 51 and cannot afford to die yet, with two young children around the place! When I was ill I was convinced I would die, but am most happy that I now am on the road to recovery. I shall miss Hoppner and I very much fear that Hearne has not long to live either. He is very broken down these days. On a happier note, Edridge has rented a house near us which is good company for me in the summers at Merry Hill.

110

I have been encouraging him to follow my custom of landscape painting, as he complains how his portrait and miniature work is getting him down. We had a very pleasant day out which resulted in a charming picture by my old friend of a certain Singer's farm, near us.

While we were both sketching I was more easily able to confide in him, firstly about my worries at Bethlem. They have decided not to build the new hospital in Islington but in Southwark, a damp spot which I definitely do not recommend after shivering in Moorfields for so long. How long will it be until we actually move into the new building? This is bad news indeed. I gather it is something to do with the terms of the trust. Our existing building belongs to the City of London and can only be exchanged for another building in its possession, or another site, as in this case. The Islington site could not be swapped and therefore was too expensive for us. One of the inmates of Bethlem, Tilly Matthews, was allowed to go in for the competition to design the new building; more to keep him and his relatives happy than that anyone expected him to win it. What a palaver there was when he didn't win, however. The governors were all up in arms on one side or the other and it was hard to remain objective. Really, if he expected to win against the best architects in the land, he certainly is mad.

Then there is all this business about my treatment by the Queen over the King's madness. I was called in finally (that is, before I became ill myself) but was only allowed to visit conjointly with Simmons; they say that the Bethlem label sticks to me too closely. I think Simmons a fool, so it goes hard with me that I have to attend always with him as my mentor. Truthfully, neither of us really knows what we can do for the King. I fear there is no cure this time. The Prince Regent, my companion for a short time in my life, behaves badly, trying to take on powers which are not his. He hates his father and it is no wonder as they are very unalike in character. It is so bad for the country to know that there is all this squabbling at the top, and of course rumour is rife.

'I am so glad,' I said to Edridge, 'that my sons and daughter do not hate me,' and there were tears in my eyes when I thought of how sweet Henry has been, particularly since he is surely the one who would have a grudge against me if anyone did. Edridge is very fond of *his* son Henry too, and agreed that it was a great blessing to have children one is close to. He is good to confide in as he is fundamentally an optimist and therefore tends to look on things from that angle and reassure one about one's deepest worries.

Madness pursues me even when I am at Merry Hill. In October the local overseer of the poor came to me one morning about a man in his care. I was less than happy as I had planned a sketching outing. The autumnal weather promised well and it might be the last time this year we could go out and lunch on the dry grass in the sun. However, I went with a fairly good grace to see the man, who was raving and trying to harm himself. The poor man: I think I remember him working in the nearby inn as an ostler not so long ago, totally in his right wits. But apparently he witnessed a terrible accident in the stable yard, someone was trampled by a horse, I don't know the details.

I asked the tailor to call and measure him for a strait waistcoat, and the fool came here instead of to the Poor House and disturbed the family at breakfast. Finally we got the man away to town and I hope to Bethlem. I was most put out as I had to go in myself too and my best sketching day was missed. How many times in my life has this sort of thing happened! This should by rights have been a free day for me.

The only bright spot in my doctoring has been the recovery of Lord Lyttleton, who has been in my care this year after a prolonged bout of melancholia. This has given

112

a fillip to my practice, as I am able to mention his cure to some of my more well connected patients' relatives. Soane, the architect and art collector, introduced me to Lyttleton, so I am grateful to him, though I do not like the collections that Soane himself has made in his town house, or his country place Pitshanger Manor. In London he has a huge sarcophagus for instance; a very gloomy looking lump of a thing. He is immensely proud of it, however.

1813

Thomas's diary

Bob has been ordained, which has given us both much pleasure, and particularly Hannah. However my greatest delight this year was in Henry who was given 100 guineas by the British Institution for his picture *The disgrace of Wolsey*. What a picture; the expressions on the disgraced Cardinal's face and those who surround him are beyond compare. It is wise of him to choose the path of history painting. If he can sell pictures like he has this one it is the way forward, according to the Academy and the powers that be. Landscape has always been well down the list of importance in their eyes.

I am most proud of my artist son, even though I think back to the time that I tried to stop him becoming an artist. He never alludes to it, which is a relief, nor indeed thinks of it I am sure. We are very close and spend many hours talking art and looking at my collections. He should be able to make his living at history painting, especially if the State grows more inclined to buy these pictures for town halls and the like. I am resolved whenever I get the chance to talk up this idea, especially with people like Beaumont, not that he is likely to change the public's mind overnight. Henry is also a portraitist, having done a good portrait of me in pastels and one of Hearne in oils. Maybe that would be more lucrative, but not highly regarded by the Academy of course. Edridge has done well from portraits, even though the Academy turn up their noses at

114

many of his pictures. If Henry could only do as well as Edridge has.

I have been iller than ever this year, though 1812 was a good year in one respect, with Napoleon at last defeated in Russia. Yet the war drags on and prices are high. There has been much wrecking of farm machinery and riots which have upset everyone, and Hannah was afraid to come out to Bushey this year. I pointed out firstly that machine wreckers were hung if caught, and secondly that no one had reported anything near Bushey, but she was still nervous. She hates me to be late of an evening, especially when it gets dark. She fears both for me and for herself. I think I could defend myself against a man with a pitch fork and I told her so! She was less sure, because my limp would make it hard for me.

My illness started with an abscess and I feared for my life. She was very sweet, prayed and wept at my bedside to such an extent that I was forced to send her away. It depressed me so much and hardly helped my recovery. Tom came when he could to see me, but the other two could not come very often, busy as they were in their separate fields. Sally is always sweet and played music to soothe me with the drawing door open and my bedroom door wide as well, when I was still confined to bed.

I was told to take on less work after the illness, but it is hard to do when I have a reputation to maintain. Holmes is about to retire from Brooke House and I begin now to realise how difficult it is to replace someone like that, dependable and, for his class, intelligent. I will not continue to attract the gentry and the aristocracy as clients for my madhouses if I cannot ensure that everything goes smoothly when I am not there. I shall begin interviewing likely replacements next week and must just pray there will be someone among them whom I like and trust.

Henry is courting a Miss Douglas now; she seems more

agreeable than Julia, but he is still quite young. Tom's fiancée Sarah is a steady girl: her father is treasurer of the Foundling Hospital and an old acquaintance of mine. Bob is hoping to marry Frederick's sister Charlotte, who is quieter than Julia. I hope their marriages are as long-lasting and happy as mine has been to Hannah, despite our differences. My illnesses have brought us closer together of late and I appreciate everything she has done for me and the family. I shall be glad if three sons are off my hands and maybe Sally too will marry before long. She is now a winsome 19.

The news of Turner is as usual both infuriating and fascinating. Farington says he is now speaking of the Academy as his own; at all events he defends it against all comers. The lectures which he has started to give are, however, apparently inaudible. This does not seem to matter so much, as he prints them out later and they are read and considered good. His picture *Snowstorm: Hannibal crossing the Alps* of last year created quite a furore. I was intrigued to note that it seems to be based on a Cozens picture of Hannibal, so I took some pride in having introduced him to Cozens's work, most of which he used to criticise under his breath, even while copying it. Some said they couldn't even see Hannibal in Turner's version, though his elephant is just visible in the distance. It is mostly a picture of storm and sunshine with some tiny people at the bottom who seem to be killing each other in a muddly sort of darkness. Henry pointed out that it is called *Snowstorm*, before the rest of the title. He says he likes it. However, when our old dog died, Henry went out and bought a fierce guard dog and said, ' We are going to call it Mallord, after you know who!'

It was an expensive breed but I am rich at the moment, having been given £500 for my attendances on the King. I

116

don't consider that this was too much, as I have attended in him ten times in the last year and have been consulted by letter about him too.

He is quite blind now, to add to the tragedy, and we were able to enter the room without his knowing it. I did not like it because I felt it was spying, but the other doctors, Bailley and Halford, thought it better to be able to observe him unnoticed. He talks to himself and sings, sometimes using language which is quite shocking for a king, but then that is nothing new to me after hearing some extraordinary things from my titled and untitled patients over the years.

I liked him very much, in the moments of sanity which seemed to shine through. It is a terrible affliction for a good man and a good king. I fear, however, that he will not recover this time and there is little we can do beyond what we do already. I feel for the Queen who is white-haired with worry now and has had so many children, twice the number my dear Hannah has had to go through with.

I often think of those words in *King Lear*, 'Let me not be mad, not mad, sweet heaven.' I couldn't agree more heartily.

The new building of Bethlem is at last getting erected but it will take a year or two before it is done. Meanwhile we struggle on with the terrible leaky, freezing building, which I loathe more bitterly with every year that passes. Haslam, too, does nothing but moan about it. I have been much exercised in my mind about York Asylum, which is now run by some servants who used to be with us in Bethlem. It turns out that a local magistrate by the name of Higgins started to investigate the place after an inmate's wife complained of his treatment there. The governors have denied there is trouble but there are wild stories of the rape and murder of some inmates. I thank God there was no such trouble at Bethlem, though I never liked Mr and Mrs King who are in control in York, and feel they may have turned

117

a blind eye to what was going on. I would be interested to know how they got a job like that up there. It is a long step from servant to manager.

But to come back to more interesting topics, Turner has apparently been quite ill, though he is only 38, but he does not spare himself, they say, always travelling or working all hours of the night and day. I often think about Tom Girtin and wonder what he would be doing were he alive today. Life is so unfair. Sometimes I think Henry may go the same way, as he hasn't been well at times and I have feared a consumptive disorder. One of my colleagues pronounced him fighting fit, so I can only hope that he is right. Henry makes nothing of it and says he is perfectly well, so I do not like to talk more of it.

Cotman has been heard of again; he has produced a set of miscellaneous etchings, mainly of architectural and anti-quarian subjects, which he thinks will be a good selling point now antiquarianism is so much in fashion. I do hope this will be the case. He does not seem to achieve the success he deserves. But then who does in this life of ours? The next life will presumably make up for injustices in this. Hannah certainly believes that.

Another interesting thing to note from last year was John Varley coming to paint my portrait, which made me look more approachable than some pictures of me done by my sons. I seem, as Hannah noted, about to speak. Indeed Varley was entertaining me with his fun as I sat, and probably I was speaking as he drew my mouth. He used the graphic telescope which Cornelius his brother invented. It is an intriguing device! I was glad he wanted to paint me; I take it as a tribute to what I have done for him in the past.

It was good to see him again and have a good long chat to him over a day or so. My goodness, how he can talk! He told me that the members of the Water Colour Society are not selling as well as they did at first and they are going to

118

change its name from this year to Painters in Oils and Water Colours. He agreed with me that it was sad to have to give way before the oil painting lobby, but there it was. He was ever sensible, old John Varley. I hope it does better under its new name and he has enough to feed his many children, which keep coming. He has made good, but he never seems to be very rich. He is always too generous a soul. They say he is always in debt, but he did not ask me for money.

1814

Thomas's diary

My darling Henry is dead!

Even as I write that word it still doesn't seem to mean anything, even now after several months have elapsed. It hurts all the more as he seemed to be at the beginning of an illustrious career. His *Disgrace of Wolsey* was followed swiftly by *Othello*, both stupendous pictures by any standards.

His illness ran its course so quickly that I was not prepared for the end. Needless to say I asked all my doctor friends for advice and several of them saw him, but there was no hope, I could see it in their eyes.

Hannah has been prostrated and sleeps much of the time. It is her way of coping with it, but it is hard for the family and I have had to try and do more with Jack and Alexander who are only 12 and 11 and cannot be left to the servants and Sally all the time. There seems a great hole in the middle of the family where Henry was, and long and bitterly have I gone over in my mind the differences we two have had and the beatings I gave him as a boy when he would not amend his spellings and would not try with his Latin.

Thank God at least I was prevailed on to let him work at his art and that he didn't die at sea, absent and unhappy. At least he died in my arms with the family around him. He found it hard to go; he looked out onto the sunny garden and said, 'If only I could go on with my art.' I wept the more.

Tom has been a great help; he is always steady and calm. Bob talks of God's taking Henry to his bosom, but I don't find it very helpful and when I see the boys playing cricket out on the lawns of Merry Hill, I still look for Henry either fielding at the edge of the lawn or laughing as he stands at the crease.

I try to keep my mind off all this and concentrate on my private practice which is expanding all the time: I have two duchesses on my books! Indeed I wear myself out riding miles and miles. It is good when the weather is fair, and I still get down and try to sketch the places of the most beauty, but my heart has not really been in it. I tear the paper at last and say, aloud sometimes, for I am alone, 'What's the point when I can never draw or paint as well as Henry, who can never pick up brush or pencil again.'

I have also been immersing myself as much as I can in the alterations I am having done still to this place, making it bigger, ironically, just as my family shrinks.

Our only happiness is the knowledge that Napoleon is safely imprisoned in Elba and the wars are over. Many people want to travel and take up the Grand Tour again. I can't say it has ever appealed to me, but I wish Henry could have made it. No doubt our dear friend Turner will be off as soon as ever he can, seeking out his mountains, his avalanches and his bloody sunsets over the sea.

My theory about him, which I was just expounding to Edridge last night (anything to get off the subject of Henry's death) is that all the sadness and violence of his mother and her final fate comes out in his gloomier and more tragic pictures. Edridge told me I had said that before, which made me feel as if I am going senile. Turner, Edridge says, adds rhymes to his pictures in the Academy catalogue which are part of some wonderful saga he has supposedly written. I can't remember offhand what he calls it, but it sounds pretentious enough. They are always ominous in tone, too.

I fancy someone else wrote them, as he certainly never seemed to have much of a literary gift when I knew him, though he would talk the hind leg off a donkey if one let him. Maybe he has picked up some education by mixing with the likes of Egremont and Essex. You never know.

Farington reported that Constable, who sat next to Turner at some Academy dinner, told Farington afterwards that Turner had a wonderful range of mind, but was totally uncouth. I thought about the 'wonderful range' a good deal after I heard that remark. I suppose he was always a keen learner and taught himself most of what he knows. I know he can talk interestingly these days, although it's hard to dismiss from one's mind his accent and the poor expression of his thoughts at times.

I have actually seen Turner's latest, which he calls *Frosty morning*. They say the chilly looking girl in it is his own elder child. I do not care for it very much, though I have to admit it is at least not too gloomy and swirling in mist for a change. Apparently the coach in the background is the one on which he was riding when he thought of the picture. Maybe from the window he saw just such a scene of peasants standing by the side of the road looking chilled to death.

Hannah has given up her flower pictures since Henry died, a pity in one way; it might have helped her to deal with her grief. She has taken to reading more of the novels which she and Sally indulge in. Sally swears by a Miss Austen, and is persuading Hannah to try her. I have heard good reports of her work, but women cannot know much of the great world, so I would be interested to know what she writes about – needlework and suchlike perhaps!

Sally is courting another Henry, Henry Earle. This is not really a suitable match but Hannah has not taken much notice of the courtship and I do not like to interfere with Sally's happiness too much, after what happened with Henry. Sometimes if one puts no bars in the way, the child will come round to sense of their own accord; that is what my wise friends tell me.

Daughters are in some ways more of a worry than sons. I can't help feeling that one of the reasons she encourages him is because she wishes to abandon this house of sorrow, although she would deny it. The burden of caring for her mother does fall largely on her in the day, and the charge of the smaller boys too. Servants cannot do everything.

She is very caring to me, too, and always tries to make me take a little wine of an evening, but I tell her it no longer agrees with me since my last illness. She says, 'You grow too thin, Father,' but I just shake my head.

I sometimes wonder how much longer I can carry on with my work load and my family, my houses, my pictures, my lads. It's been a good full life but I am tired now. I am finding my Bethlem duties particularly very irksome, especially as we are still waiting to move into better accommodation.

*

Alavoine, the steward at Bethlem hospital, is having an interview with Monro in his office.

'You mean you refused to let Wakefield see round the wards?' Monro asks down what seems to Alavoine his formidable nose.

'I thought it best, sir. You never know what these interfering busybodies want. I just said, sir, that I would have to get a Governor from the committee sir, to be with him. That was right, wasn't it, sir?'

'Well yes, in theory it was, but you can see, man, that it does not look good, if he then has to reapply to come with a Member of Parliament as well as a Governor.'

'I wasn't to know that, was I sir? It was a pity, sir, that I couldn't locate a member of the committee. I did try. Indeed I did. Ask Mr Haslam.'

'Yes, yes, yes.' Monro shuffles his papers. He reflects that he, too, would have tried to keep Wakefield out. It's a pity that the staff at St Luke's let him see round their hospital without any trouble, on the same day. It looks as if we have something to hide. Which, he thinks to himself, indeed we have, or we had before Wakefield and the MP saw it: Norris chained to a pole so he can hardly sit up or lie down. Haslam's fault of course, because he would not administer opium so the violence would be lost in dopiness, and not before Norris had attacked several people.

Monro, looking up, sees the slight body of Alavoine trembling. 'Sit down, man, I shan't tell the Governors it was your fault. The point is that Wakefield is of the new school, like these people up in York. Have you heard of Higgins who is investigating some claim of cruelty?'

'I have indeed, sir. They do say the physician there was forced to leave, sir.'

'Yes, indeed,' Monro replies dryly.

'It's all in the newspapers, sir, with a picture by an artist they took with them. Of Norris, you know.' Alavoine, now less nervous, was getting voluble.

'Well, we must weather the storm now it's come. Also look to our treatment of Tilly Matthews; he's a trouble-maker if ever there was one and his family insist he is not mad.'

'They should see him sometimes, sir.'

'I agree, I too have seen him at his worst, but unfortunately Wakefield seems to have taken up his cause along with Norris's. That will be all, Alavoine.' He did not add, 'Look to yourself, Wakefield has it in for you too.' What, after all, could a steward do against the might of a friend of Wilberforce's, a member of a reforming group with power behind him.

He watched the man leave. 'Thank you, sir.'

Thank me for what? Thomas ruminates gloomily. You

124

will lose your job whatever I say. He feels both exhausted and angry, also afraid.

Thomas's diary

I fear I may have to let Tom take the Bethlem job, but what will I do for money?

If I talk money to Hannah her eyes glaze over; her only suggestion ever is to sell my pictures. This is a possibility, of course, or at least some of them, but I hate the way she thinks they are expendable just because she does not understand my passion and has never liked having all the young artists about the place.

I never show her what I do on my travels, the sketches which I work up in the evenings. I think she considers them mere blots and scribbles. None of the family save my beloved Henry ever took much notice of what I did on those lines. It is just Papa's little hobby, nor are they very interested in my collection and they always groan if I get out Gainsborough's camera lucida to show my friends. I suppose to them it is like the telling of a well-worn joke. They feel embarrassed and bored.

Having said that, Jack and Alexander have shown some interest lately, though I wonder if Sally has not set them on to do it, to try and cheer me up. They are nice boys, though I think on the wild side, just as Henry was.

I have had the portraits Henry did of the family framed and set up in the drawing room, which pleases Hannah, though she starts crying when she sees them. I am very anxious to get hold of *The disgrace of Wolsey* and *Othello*.

Constable has written a kind letter to us. Of course Turner has not, though to be fair he hardly knew Henry. The lads, especially Hunt, has been very sweet when they come over, but sometimes I have dark thoughts. Why

125

should he, a cripple, survive and my Henry, who had such a wonderful physique as well as such obvious talent, die? Can it be the will of God?

I try to accept it and I pray and listen to sermons in church, but it doesn't really touch me; though I think religion *has* helped Hannah. When she tells me to go to church more or pray for God's grace, I tell her I am soothed most by God's creation around me as I journey; the lakes, trees and fields of our beautiful England, as yet untouched down here in the south, though the new towns of Manchester and Liverpool are full of horrors. Slums and poverty and no air: at least the poor round here can breathe fresh air and see trees and flowers. Aye, and a lot of mud too, Henry would probably have said.

Hearne has been strange about Henry. Although he was fond of the lad in his way, he has not said much. I think Hearne has his own worries and has been complaining of ill health these last few years. Of course he never married, but still it has been hard to bear his silence on the subject closest to my heart. He is, instead, full of oaths about Turner. 'Do you know what that pipsqueak has done, he only put in a picture for the British Institution competition *eleven days late*. He had no business to go in for the competition anyway, it's for young artists, and he's nearly forty!'

'So what was the picture?' I asked.

'*Apullia in search of Apullius vide Ovid!* Or some such nonsense. It's a Claude impression, that he's so good at, or fancies he is anyway. Beaumont and Payne Knight were spitting with rage.'

'Can't they merely say he cannot enter it because it's late?'

'I suppose so, but they know the newspapers will catch on to it. He only makes up stupid titles like that to cock a snook at their classical educations.'

126

'Why does he bother?' I asked. 'He does very well anyway.'

'Oh, he can't bear their disdain. He's like a child! Do you remember years ago, Beaumont attacked his imitation of Claude, said it wanted colour or some such; everyone says he did this to prove he could out-Claude the master. He certainly nurses grudges well. I hope *you* never did anything or said anything which might have upset him, Thomas.'

'I'm small fry,' I said, smiling a little. 'All he does is to put an ironic twist on the words "the good Doctor" which he always calls me when we meet. I don't mind. I know he is aware of many favours I have done him.' I did not mention what I did to help him over Mrs Turner, because I have never mentioned it to anyone. I shall certainly have to face up to that one on Judgement Day. As it is, it often comes to haunt me on sleepless nights. Who knows what he and his father would have done with the mother if I had not helped them? Would she have stayed behind with them and upset Turner's career as best she could? There's every betting he would have left her behind whatever I did. However, that doesn't really make me feel any better.

Farington told me the other day that Turner has built a new home for himself at Twickenham, to be called Solus Lodge: amusing that he can call attention to his own loneliness so obviously. Farington, however, says it isn't loneliness he wants to stress, it is going it alone. According to Farington, who made a special journey to see it, it has elements of Fetcham about it. I would be flattered if I really believed it based on my house.

*

Thomas Monro is visiting Bethlem, an extra visit which seems required since all the trouble with Wakefield. Haslam

127

is there to meet him, surly as ever, but with a frightened look in his eyes.

'Do you wish to make a tour of the wards today, sir?' he asks, realising what is in Thomas's thoughts.

'Good idea, Haslam. Have you the book of new patients on you? Let's see, how many have we at present, and what of Norris? Is he being kept apart in his own room?'

'Yes, Norris is free to move about his own room, sir. He has no furniture, because as you know, sir, he destroys it. The bed is moved in at night so he can sleep. So far he has not damaged that.'

Thomas did not say what he was thinking, that all this amounted to was locking the stable door after the horse had bolted.

The smell as usual hit him as he went through the doors, along with the cold. If he liked Haslam better he might have sympathised with him in his plight living there all the time.

He had not been round the wards for a long time now and he cursed himself that he had not. The few mad people who were dosed with opium were sitting or lying quietly in their straw; the next room was noisier, with several singing and some shouting. Quite a few of these were chained. They took little notice of him, he realised, partly because many of them did not recognise him, for unless they were ill or new he hardly saw them. One man shook his fist. There were remains of food on the floor and Thomas directed that these should be removed. 'We shall have rats in here if we are not careful.'

'Oh, we have those already, sir,' the warder, Baines, said with what seemed like satisfaction. He smelt suspiciously of gin, but Thomas said nothing to him. He knew the difficulties by now of getting sober men and women to work as warders at all.

One man was moving slowly, even majestically, about

128

with an old rag on his head. 'He thinks he's Bonaparte,' the warder said sniggering. 'Hey, Boney!' The man made an imperial gesture, which sent Baines off again, guffawing this time.

Thomas was trying to imagine himself into the role of inspector. 'We should have these chains off, Haslam.'

'That means we have to dose them, sir.'

'Well, do it!' he said, knowing that Haslam probably would not, and if challenged later would say he could not remember receiving the order. He decided he would write it down in the log book downstairs, so at least it would not be seen as his fault if Haslam went his own way after he had gone.

One of the female patients leered up at Baines.

'I hope there is no access to the female wards at night except by the female warders.'

'Oh no, sir.' Baines was sanctimonious.

Thomas gave Haslam a sharp look, as much as to say, 'Keep an eye on Baines.'

'Now, is there anyone I should see in my room?' he asked when they concluded the miserable tour, and Monro had written in the log book.

'I think not today, sir. They are all fit, or as fit as they ever will be. Unless you think that Hearnshaw should be bled.'

'We'll see how he goes on. Keep a detailed account of his behaviour for when I come next.'

'I certainly will, sir.'

'Yes, we must be vigilant,' Thomas said, rising to go. He knew from Haslam's expression that he knew what Monro meant.

Well, it isn't a palace, but who said it ever was likely to be? he asked himself and he shivered as he went down the steps. Money is the key and there isn't enough. He shrugged his shoulders and got into his carriage. Really it would be a relief never to see that place again; even though today wasn't as bad as in the season when the inmates were vomited and defecated. Then it was hardly bearable to go in at all.

1815

Hannah and Thomas are seated in her boudoir in the Adelphi house, he with a newspaper in his hand.

'This is Wakefield's letter about Bethlem. I would like you to read it, my dear.'

'You read it to me, I know from your looks that it contains bad news.' The tea she is sipping tastes bitter in her mouth.

'I'm afraid it does. He certainly seems able to wake more than fields; he is out to waken the conscience of England. But I think you must read it yourself,' and he hands her the paper.

Hannah barely takes in the pun, but when she does she reflects how like her Thomas that is; a sort of grim humour in the face of adversity.

When she has finished it, he looks at her inquiringly. 'I don't quite understand it,' she falters.

'Unfortunately Wakefield inspected Bethlem and saw Norris, whom I spoke to you about before, you remember. He was chained to a pole by his bed in what Wakefield calls unacceptable and sordid conditions. Haslam and I are blamed, among others, but I think we two principally. Yes, principally, and I am senior to him, so . . .' and he gestures.

'So what does it mean, this horrible man poking and prying?'

'I suspect it means the loss of my job. I only hope to God

Tom may inherit it, as he well expects to. There will be a House of Commons Select Committee inquiry, it seems.'

'And you who have been called in by the Queen and her ministers for your opinion on King George's madness! They couldn't force you out!'

Thomas is touched by his wife's partisan approach to his problem. 'Take no notice, my dear, I am probably seeing things too blackly this morning. I have to admit as the sun rose I thought, "The sun rises, I face the committee, I am forced to resign. They are all as inevitable as each other." But perhaps that is too bleak a picture. Haslam may have to take the full blame, as I feel he should. He has always ignored what I tell him to do. I think I have told you before that he never doses the violent inmates and is then forced to chain them, to stop them attacking each other or the warders.'

But he thinks to himself, Haslam in his turn will try to make me look responsible; he is no fool in that respect.

Hannah has bad news of her own, but has not dared communicate it. As Thomas rises to go, she decides she must. 'Don't bother to say goodbye to Sally today, she is in her room and does not want to be disturbed.'

'That is not like Sal. What can be the matter?'

'It's her Henry, you know that she is engaged,' and Hannah starts to cry.

'Well, she says so; I don't set much store by that account and I do not find him suitable.'

'I should have said, she *was* engaged. He has apparently broken it off; so you need not continue to disapprove,' and she almost smiled amidst her tears.

'And to what do we owe this relief from adversity?'

She was silent.

'Ah, I see he has got wind of some possible disgrace to our family. You knew before I showed you the newspaper letter, I think.'

132

'People talk, Thomas.' She gets up and pats him awkwardly. 'I will try to be strong and help you. Try not to grieve.'

'Now Hannah, do not exaggerate. Have I shown any sign of grieving? And as to Sally's news, I am very pleased she is rid of him. She will see it like that too, soon I hope.' It is his turn to pat his wife. 'Now cheer up. We'll live.'

'It's just that you have hardly bothered to admit to yourself that Tom has provided us with a grandchild; it should have been such wonderful news, and somehow it is swallowed up in all this worry and fret.'

'It's good news of course, Hannah, but this must be sorted out before everything else. At least I haven't joined the ranks of Bethlem inmates yetawhile!'

'But your migraines are worse, I know that, and your indigestion. You must try to rest more, Thomas.'

'I will try,' he says but not in a voice that promises results. 'It is such an irony that we are about to move into the new Bethlem building which will solve many of the inmates' and staff's problems, but just at the moment it is making much more work.'

'I am so sorry, Thomas,' is all poor Hannah can say as she wipes her eyes and blows her nose.

He smiles at her as he prepares to leave. 'Don't worry, we'll manage somehow with the school fees for Jack and Alex, even if I have to sell my precious pictures!'

'No, Thomas, you mustn't do that.'

He raises an eyebrow at that, for it is usually her cry that he should. He does not, however, say what rises to his lips, 'So my being in trouble has some advantages to it!'

'Take the carriage, Thomas,' she calls after him, but she cannot hear his reply.

She rings the bell for the servant and starts to tidy up her possessions a little, muttering to herself the while: 'If you ask me these mad people would be better dead. In some

133

cases. What use are they to anyone? I'd like to see this Wakefield dealing with that Norris in his own house. He'd be the first to tie him back up, if Norris didn't kill him first.'

When the servant has gone, she sits and looks at her own reflection. Her own squint and how it worsens, which is usually at the top of her list, is now overtaken by Sally's woe, Thomas's possible disgrace and poor health, his concern for his friend Hearne who is fading and worst of all something which she doesn't want to think about: the accusation that Jack has been found drinking at Harrow. He is always such a nice cheery lad with such a frank face. Hannah thinks they must have muddled him with another boy.

Thomas had told her this news last week, and she couldn't believe it. It seems however, that Thomas does. How could he believe that about his own son? Hannah fears that he will be very stern and beat Jack more than he ever beat Henry. And how heartsick he had been when he looked back on those beatings after Henry's death.

At least he had sympathised with her when she had wept over Jack. She had said she couldn't believe it of her own child and he had repeated the old joke, 'Poor Hannah, all your geese are swans.'

Of course in the case of his geese, Turner had become a very big swan indeed. She knows Thomas was secretly delighted he had helped the youth on his way, even though she still cannot bear to see the man even now. Well, she thinks as she turns from her looking glass, he does not often come near the Adelphi or Bushey nowadays, but when he does I always eat out of the range of his disgusting table manners. She laughs to herself, even now on this terrible morning, when she thinks about their dog Mallord. I only wish Turner knew what his namesake was like, she thinks, opening Thomas's room where he still has some Turners on the wall. Slopping his food in the bowl and chewing bones, he is exactly like JMW when he does that. Visitors always laugh when she tells them.

Thomas's diary

Well, I have survived the House of Commons Committee but only just. To do him justice, George Rose, who conducted it, has made it clear to the Governors that Haslam and I must be able to defend ourselves in writing before they make any decision about getting rid of us or keeping us on.

To tell you the truth I have no heart for it any more. Tom has been here a lot in the past months and we have discussed the future for him too. I very much hope that if I have to go, Tom will be voted in in my place. I shan't be sorry to go if it comes to that, but it is the fashion of my going that I shall hate.

At the moment I *feel* any slights to me, whether by highborn people or servants, and I probably imagine some of it. Hannah certainly says that I do. I feel a broken man, and not even the final defeat of Napoleon by Wellington, at the glorious battle of Waterloo in which some of our family fought, can waken me from a feeling of loss and doom.

I think that I defended myself pretty well at the hearing in the House of Commons; after all it is Haslam who has consistently neglected his duties, but I am made a scapegoat because I have the senior post. I realised that that would be the way of it. I told the committee that there are only four keepers at Bethlem and therefore not enough to allow the dangerous patients to be free of restraints. This means they must be chained or doped. It is Haslam who orders the chains, not I. He does not believe in strait waistcoats which tie their hands, as they must care for their own bodily functions and need their hands free for this reason. After all there

135

are about 123 lunatics in there. Four keepers are not enough but I do not hold the purse strings. I have told the Governors enough times that we need more and better staff.

The recent move of the hospital to Southwark has, of course, changed some of the conditions for the better, but I always thought the new place they chose marshy and therefore not healthy for the patients. I made it clear I did not choose the new spot and was disappointed it was not to be Islington after all. There are various other problems: the baths have been put in a very awkward position in the new building, for instance, and only men can now bathe after their usual purging and vomiting in May and June. So the women remain filthy.

The committee questioned the use of purging and vomiting. I had to admit that Haslam has never been keen on the vomiting of patients, but it has always been the treatment preferred by my grandfather and father and I know no better one.

'Did Fowler, one of the patients, die after coming out of a cold bath?' was their next question.

I told them I didn't recollect this happening, but I am only there on Mondays and Wednesdays, I said. I didn't think cold baths in summer were injurious, but on the contrary were welcomed by the patients who needed cleaning after treatment which included vomiting and defecation.

They asked me whether my private patients were purged and vomited in the same way. I said they were bled and physicked.

They nodded at that, as much as to say, So they are not purged and vomited. 'Are they chained like the Bethlem inmates?'

'No,' I said, 'there is no necessity as I provide plenty of assistants to restrain them, which are not provided at Bethlem. In any case if a gentleman was put into irons he would not like it.'

136

There was a sudden hush. I had not realised how the committee would react to that simple statement. They shook their heads and looked askance and Rose took me up sharply. 'So you think a gentleman would feel being fettered more than a common lunatic would?'

'Yes, assuredly. Some of the lunatics knew very little better in their former lives than the straw they live in now. Norris is a ferocious being, a brute; he has hardly any sensibilities at all. He has bitten one patient's finger off and attacked warders on several occasions.'

'Nonetheless he should not be chained to a post so he cannot even turn over in his bed nor move from it, with a twenty-eight-pound weight on him if he stands up, unable to move his arms at all.'

'I have never chained any of my patients. Mr Haslam sees to that.'

'But you saw him chained on your rounds?'

'I see patients who are admitted or need special observation in a room near the front door. I do not go into the wards.'

'So you do not make rounds?'

'I leave that to Mr Haslam. It is his job. If he needs to report to me, he does so.'

'But you knew of Norris?'

'I knew of him. I had also met him and tried to treat him. Although restrained he swore and spat at me, trying to bite too. He had wounded various keepers; there was very little we could do to restrain him.'

'Yet he was beaten by the keeper Davies and his arm broken.'

'Only in self-defence, I believe.'

'Davies was often intoxicated and according to reports often found on the women's side of the hospital.'

'I have no knowledge of that.' I know Baines is drunken and lecherous, but I did not say so.

137

'Was it right to keep Norris in the general ward? Should he not have been kept separately?'

'Yes, it would have been better, if there was money for this allotted by the Governors.' I did not add that this was a big 'if'. 'In my private practice a man like this would be kept apart. But I am glad to say I have had no other case in all my history of employment with the insane such as Norris's. He was the nearest thing to an animal that I have ever come across.'

I wished heartily that Norris could be brought in to show those mealy-mouthed puritans who were so superciliously questioning me what a madman really is like. They'd be the first to run behind the door to get away!

The worst of it was that they got the new steward, who came after the Governors got rid of Alavoine, to say that I didn't always visit on Mondays and Wednesdays, which is a lie. He did admit that he might not have seen me, as I visited only the front rooms, where I saw the new patients and anyone who needed me. How can he tell whether I keep to my timetable if he is at the back of the building? Everything is at sixes and sevens with the move anyway and there is also a new matron. No one knows who is doing what until it all settles down. What a time to investigate the place!

I was very relieved when the questioning was over and Haslam's turn came. I imagine that he blamed me as much as he could, but I hear he blamed Crowther the surgeon too, and I had also admitted to the committee that Crowther is often intoxicated. I know that Haslam told them he had wanted to put Norris into two rooms unchained, but the Governors originally insisted he should be chained. No one is really taking responsibility for Norris's condition, this is what it boils down to. In fact Bethlem is now considered by everyone I meet to be on a par with a dungeon in a medieval castle.

138

Haslam was very lengthy and arrogant in his answers, which does not surprise me. But it was hard that no one smiled or acknowledged me as I left the intimidating room the committee was held in. I realised as I came out how tense I was; I seemed to ache all over and I could hardly limp to my carriage.

The next Governors' meeting will be next year, but I shall be writing my defence immediately, to exonerate myself. I could not bear to feel that I left under a cloud. What would my father and grandfather have thought of me? Yet I have done everything and omitted nothing that they did. This is a bolt from the blue. I am 57 but feel 77.

It does not help that my friend Hearne is very ill and in poverty, and that my friend Alexander is also ailing. Luckily what remains of my family is well, especially Hannah who has become a different, and I have to admit a much nicer, woman in the last 12 months. She has reiterated her opinion that whatever happens I must not sell my pictures. I kissed her heartily for that.

The day I got back from the committee I had the servants pour me a very full, very hot bath and I symbolically scrubbed off all the criticisms that had accrued to me that day. Hannah asked me about it, but I only told her a little; assuring her I was going to write my defence and all, after all, would be well. What is the point of worrying her further?

Later that evening Farington called, full of art world gossip which I found strangely calming in its effect, although it is not calm in itself. Luckily he was so full of it he didn't ask me about the committee, and perhaps he genuinely knew nothing of it. It would not interest him. My doctoring is nothing to him.

He told me that a pamphlet had appeared and no one knew who had written it, though, he said, putting his finger to his nose, they suspect Fawkes, who has no time for

139

classically educated connoisseurs like Beaumont and Payne Knight. The pamphlet mocked those whose only standard is old pictures, and of course, though Turner wasn't mentioned by name, he was meant to represent the new school of ideas. We know how thick Turner and Fawkes are.

'Beaumont is mortified, they say. He senses his power is at an end and he told me he's never going to commit himself on Turner again. "If people want him, they can have him," he said. I felt almost sorry for poor Beaumont. He's not such a bad old fellow.'

'He has done much financially to my certain knowledge for many struggling artists,' I said loyally.

'And you too, Monro,' Farington said, patting me on the shoulder.

'Oh, me, I haven't that sort of money,' I said.

A few weeks later Farington returned gleefully with a copy of an article by Hazlitt on Turner's work. He had ringed round the words 'his landscapes are all pictures of nothing and very like'.

'Didn't we always say so, Thomas?' and he clapped me on the back and laughed uproariously.

But somehow, criticising someone else did not make me laugh. I am too raw myself and the Royal College of Physicians has been strangely silent, which I find an alarming sign. Surely they should back me at this moment.

I hardly heard him say he was going off to show the article to Beaumont to cheer him up. If only Farington knew *I* was the one who was really drowning, but he is not the most sensitive of souls.

1816

Thomas Monro and his son Edward Thomas are sitting in front of the Bethlem hospital committee in the severe-looking boardroom, to all outward appearances quite calm, though young Tom is blinking rather rapidly. Thomas stares ahead, passively waiting to be questioned.

'Well, Dr Monro,' the chairman begins, 'we have read your defence, which you and Haslam were invited to make by the Select Committee. We have of course also read his. We will be speaking to him in a moment. However, we have decided to ask you to attend today with your son to hear our decision on these matters.'

Here it comes, Thomas thinks. He merely bows.

'We are fully and painfully aware that many of the problems thrown up by Wakefield when he visited the Hospital last year were not of your making. However, you are aware that you are the senior member of staff and that therefore you must take responsibility for what your juniors do. We have the painful job today,' and the red-faced old chairman is sweating as he says this, 'of informing you that from today you no longer hold an appointment at the hospital. However,' he adds quickly seeing that Thomas Monro is about to speak, 'we have today taken a vote not only in your case but also on the proposition that your son should succeed you as you succeeded both your father and grandfather before you in the position of Head Physician.

'We are therefore glad to tell you, Dr Monro,' and he

141

turns to Tom, 'that you have been voted in as Physician to Bethlem Hospital.'

Tom and Monro stop holding their breaths, but, though the chairman reaches forward and shakes hand affably with Tom, he returns to his desk and continues. 'However, the Select Committee were concerned that this job should no longer be in one single man's hands.' Thomas senior winces. 'And therefore it has been decided that you should share the appointment with Tuthill, a lecturer at the Royal College of Physicians and a sound man. He has already agreed to take up his post and we hope you will accept the position of joint Physician with him. Before you say anything I should point out that weekly visits by the Physicians will increase from two days a week to four, and you will visit on alternate days, namely you, Monro, on Mondays and Thursdays, and Tuthill on Wednesdays and Fridays. Thus you will have no heavier workload than your father had. You will also be operating from the new building which will make your job a lot easier than your father's has been.' He pauses. 'So that all it behoves me to do now is to extend our heartfelt thanks to you, Thomas Monro, for all your sterling work over these many years, and to communicate our regret and great sadness that it should have to end in this manner; but as you may know, our hands are tied.'

The Monros make their departure after the rest of the board have all shaken hands with them and murmured suitable phrases.

Tom can read his father's mood from the back of his neck as he walks down the stairs and is not sure what to say to him, but Monro speaks first.

'Congratulations, Tom, at least you have your employment. I was so afraid you too might lose out in this.'

'I am very sorry, as you may guess, Father, that I get this position in these miserable circumstances, and not as I should have done, on your death or retirement.'

'You're a good boy,' he says. 'Well, at least we have the satisfaction that Haslam will get a roasting. I am only sorry I could not stop for that. And now we must pick up the pieces, or at least I must. You will start with Tuthill. He is a steady hand, about twice your age, a Cambridge man and a classical scholar as far as I remember. You will have that in common.' He pauses. 'I only hope they do not intend to cut your salary in half too!' and he lets out a rusty laugh.

After this Monro says little, takes a favourite picture from the netting on the ceiling of the carriage and loses himself in contemplating it. Tom has the sense to keep his thoughts to himself.

He shuts his eyes and goes over in his mind the Tuthill business, which is a shock, but he is a sanguine person and does not expect to hate his co-physician. Nor does he expect to lose out financially. After this he thinks back over his father's defence, which he has read most recently that morning. He considers it a wonderful work, although he knows his father experienced problems in writing it, for the very reason that he had not really been accused of anything specific by the Governors. Monro therefore had to made up his own charges based on what the Select Committee had accused him of, to wit, firstly, that he was wanting in humanity to his patients, secondly, that he had pursued medical treatments indiscriminate in application, cruel in themselves and useless and injurious to the patients, and thirdly, inhumanity.

Tom remains impressed that his father had so neatly enumerated it like this – how hard that must have been! His introduction had been more personal: he had talked of the blow being so unexpected that it fell very heavy and of his painful humiliation. Nonetheless he had gone through each allegation and explained what had happened in various particular cases, and really the blame had always adhered to Haslam in these matters, not to him.

143

Poor Father, thinks Tom, glancing at him across the swaying carriage, he has suddenly shrunk physically over these last few months. It has affected him more than Henry's death, in one way. He is a man who has failed in his own eyes and that has crushed him.

Of course if they had done what the Governing Committee had always refused him because of their chronic shortage of money, that is, getting rid of imbecilic, alcoholic and plain criminal members of the staff, then he would still be there. As for the number of times he had asked for better living conditions for the inmates, I cannot remember how many times I have heard him telling us when he got home, his voice tired with talking, how little he could change the minds of those fellows on the Board of Governors. Tom hopes fervently that as a new appointee he may have a chance to change things which his father could not.

I shall stress, he thinks, that they have to spend more money if they want to get the sort of person to be a warder who is not cruel or drunken. If they pay them so little, of course they get the dregs! No doubt they will plead that they are always short of money and that they have spent so much already on the new building. What irony that Father should go just as conditions improve physically in the new place.

Well, Tom thinks, opening his eyes again and contemplating his father's figure, he is 57 now, so I haven't really been given my chance much earlier than would have been natural. He worries about money, but what about me? Sarah is expecting another baby soon and we already have darling little Edward. For a minute he allows himself to imagine little Edward as the next Physician at Bethlem, but he cannot merge his vision of his sweet little white-clothed infant with the dark brown boardroom he has just left, and gives it up with a chuckle and a sigh.

He wonders how the vote actually went, how many

people voted for Monro senior and how many against. His father must surely have wondered that as he said goodbye to each man.

The weather has turned sour, too, and he sees as he looks out that it is raining heavily. Tom switches his thoughts to the state of the world around him, as his father gets out his whisky flask and passes it over silently. It has been one of the wettest years on record so far and everyone is depressed generally, and particularly about the harvest, which is ruined. There are many beggars about because of the soldiers returning from the wars, with not enough jobs to go to. What a terrible effect peace has had, after being awaited so long. Should he try and engage his father in conversation on this topic? Despite the offer of the whisky, he decides not to.

He knows Monro is worried about Jack, too, since the boy has been threatened with being expelled from Harrow, after being found drinking in the town after hours. Tom finds it difficult to understand his brother, who is 15 and quite old enough to realise what their father is going through.

Tom knows, as they all do, that Jack wishes to pursue art as a career. His father, tied by the memory of Henry, is finding it hard to say no, but even so he won't allow it. Jack is a wild boy; even their mother, who loves her last two boys so dearly, has to admit that. Sal saw him kissing the scullery maid in the corridor last holidays. Thank God Father never heard of that, thinks Tom.

They alight from the carriage at last and enter the house. Immediately Monro looks up at the picture Henry painted of the *Disgrace of Wolsey*, which now hangs in pride of place. With a catch in his voice he says, '*Disgrace of Monro*, that is what he should have painted, had he lived.'

1817

Thomas's diary

Hearne died this year, in poverty.

I feel my part in it was not as kind and helpful as it might have been. I paid for the burial, but of course this was too late to be of any use to the man himself. I had to admit to myself that of late he irritated me and even appalled me. I am having a memorial erected in Bushey Church to him, which I hope will go some way to relieving my sense of guilt. I always admired his work and I was glad to be able to discuss it with Beaumont, who of course was at the interment and took several of us back to his London mansion afterwards for a meal. He did his best for Hearne at the end by sending a nurse to him at his own expense. Sir George has ever been generous with artists in this manner, and I take my hat off to him for it.

Beaumont's very early influence was Hearne and he has never forgotten that. He talked long and earnestly about him, and said we should do something for his son. It turns out he has one, got outside marriage of course.

I suppose one shouldn't be surprised by anything these days. It occurred to me that that might account for his odd attitude when my Henry died. But why didn't he tell me he had a son? One can't help looking back and thinking that one didn't know one's friends as well as one thought at the time, when such secrets are kept. Well, he kept it from everyone it seems, not just from me.

At Beaumont's we discussed the inevitable JMW too. He

told me that Turner's child Evalina was married this year. I hadn't realised she was old enough to be of marriageable age. It was a shock. The husband is something in the consular service, Beaumont says. She was lucky, but perhaps Turner did more for his family than it is reported he did, in the financial way at least. We discussed the picture which is supposedly of both his children, *Crossing the brook* or some such name. Beaumont calls it 'pea-green insipidity'! And I dared not disagree with him as we were eating his food in his palatial mansion; I merely nodded and hmmmed. I had actually thought it rather good when I saw it.

Turner's father is quite an old man now, over 70, anyway. He's the only one to live in Twickenham with Will apart from the housekeeper, who is related to Danby I believe. They say that Turner has got very portly these days; well, he is 42 I suppose. No longer a young man.

They say he is occupied with a large picture of the field of Waterloo, but that it shows no national pride or grandeur, but only human suffering. That certainly won't go down well when he shows it at the RA. Apparently he has visited the scene to get as much verisimilitude into the picture as possible. Beaumont snorted and said that it wouldn't look like anything but a lot of blotches anyway, so what was the point of his travelling all that way? I must say Sir George has a really long knife into Turner and there is no real reason why he should be so virulent. He seems to like to tell me in particular the latest horrors, I think because he knows I once helped Turner and he can't bear that.

He told me with a grim pleasure that JMW was unable to give his lectures at the Academy this year, because of the pressure of engagements. 'Engagements pah!' he exclaimed, 'he is busy getting all his pictures engraved so he can make a lot of money. Luckily for him the engravers manage to make more sense of the canvases than he deserves, and they sell well in the cheaper format. Do you know he has put in his will that part of the land he owns in Twickenham should go for almshouses for decaying artists? He is that all right himself, so he must know all about it!'

'Isn't the word *decayed?*' Edridge dared to put in.

'No doubt, no doubt,' Sir George laughed. 'Well, he's *decayed* too,' and he popped a huge piece of beef in his mouth.

Edridge glanced at me as much as to say, At least Turner is doing something for other artists, not just himself, which is new for him.

Beaumont, who does a lot himself, wouldn't ever admit that Turner could be equally helpful and kind. I was a little surprised myself, but then I remembered Turner was usually kind to Tom Girtin, and they say he loves children.

I feel a little decayed myself, and there is nothing that reminds one of one's mortality than the death of a close friend.

I think I shall give up Adelphi Terrace in a year or so. I need to draw in my horns with the last two boys proving rather spendthrift, and the loss of my income to Tom. I must say he has been very tactful about taking over from me, knowing how painful the wound still feels over my dismissal. He does sometimes have to ask me about the job and we both try and remain very businesslike during these sessions. Occasionally as he goes out he takes my hand and squeezes it a little and that is all the sympathy I think I can take from him. He is a good boy and a really first-rate man. I am 58 and finding it harder and harder to walk, though riding I can still do.

I wonder how long it will be before I join Hearne under the soil. Beaumont is older than me but seems hale and hearty so far. May God grant me a little longer so I can see my last two children out into the world.

Beaumont, of course, has no children and I couldn't help thinking he was lucky. I am worried about Jack, who I have decided I am going to send off to France. I hope it is a good move. With new acquaintances and surroundings he may do better than at school, though he is only 16 and Hannah feels he is still too young. But I trust the good people he will stay with and have great hopes for his future.

I have to state here that Jack has very willingly helped me lately to sort out Hearne's drawings which lay about in great abundance in his house and which no one seemed to want. The house has to be cleared before being sold. Jack was really keen, but then he loves art. I gave him one or two that he admired the most, to thank him. However, once it was done he seemed to revert to moodiness, fits of temper and saying he was bored. He goes out without telling anyone where, which causes his mother huge anxieties when he is very late back at night. I threaten him with a beating but no threats seem to affect him and I am reluctant to beat him as I did Henry, though he deserves it much more.

Poor Edridge has lost his daughter and I feel for him. His adoration is, however, for his son, and he does not speak much of his girl. It's hard therefore to offer him consolation. The only difference is that he is less bouncy in company than he was, and I thought I detected a wet eye when Beaumont talked of Turner's daughter getting married. Edridge has done a charming picture of Bushey Church including the memorial to Hearne; he did it with Hearne's own paper and pencil; a sentimental touch if you like, but I could see it meant a lot to him.

On a happier note, Tom has given us another grandson and to our delight he has called him Henry. We hope and trust he will have as many talents as his namesake and be just as dear to his parents as Henry was to us.

I hear that the man who has taken over at Bethlem from Haslam is a man called Wright. He is very interested in what they call phrenology. It involves measuring the head so you can find out more about the man's or woman's personality. They say he has started to keep the heads of the dead madmen and madwomen and cut them open to study them. I spoke to Tom about it and he thinks it is a good idea, as madness must stem from the brain, but at Bethlem they find it a ghoulish practice going on right under their noses and they do not like him.

Wright and Tuthill do not see eye to eye, Tom tells me, though whether it is because of his cutting the brains open I don't know. We Monros seem doomed to be in the midst of problems at Bethlem; if it isn't Haslam and yours truly, it is Tuthill and Wright. Well at least Tom is keeping out of it as best he can. By not visiting on the same days at Tuthill he at least does not see him, and can listen to Wright's version without interruption.

I am so glad that is behind me, even though Tom says the new building is much better than the old. I do not get the feeling that Tom enjoys the job, but he keeps his feelings from me and always tries to talk cheerfully about Bethlem. Apparently they had a visit from the Duke and Duchess of Gloucester and the Duchess of York, who were very pleased with the place! And they now have religious services there; Budd from Bridwell officiates, although Tuthill is not keen in case the religious enthusiasts among the inmates are made worse. I heartily agree with Tuthill, but it's all change at Bethlem now it seems that the liberals have got their claws into it. As for Haslam, I was profoundly shocked to hear he has *bought* himself an MD from the proceeds of selling his library. I wonder how much it cost him. Thus he can practise as a physician. Good luck to him; I should think he will prove a disastrous one!

1818

Thomas's diary

More woe; Edridge's son Henry died this July, after a short
illness. I gave my friend as much help as I could both
medically and by writing continually to him whilst he took
the boy to the West Country for his health. Edridge wrote
to me very frequently asking my advice. The journey, as I
half feared it would, made things far worse for the boy
who was in a consumption, but he also seems to have had
complications in the intestines. Edridge tried everything he
could think of and every doctor he could find. He wrote
me the most anguished letters, which were painful to read.
I think he needed an outlet for all his anxieties. In any
case it is hard to give constructive advice when one cannot
examine the patient at all. I did not know the son well but
he seems to have been an exceptional lad. He died finally
in Taunton, far from Hanwell where Edridge lives. It must
have been extremely unpleasant to have him dying in a
hotel and not in his own home. Everyone a stranger. Poor
Edridge. All this trouble for him has made me relive my
own and I bewailed my ill fortune in losing my own Henry
so young.

He keeps saying that we must see much more of each
other as there are so few of us left nowadays; but at the
moment I do not want to see him. He pulls me down at a
time when I am far from hearty myself. It will be particularly sad to see Edridge cast down, as we have always relied
on him to make us laugh at his stories and enjoy his songs

at the piano. Sally is very sad to hear her favourite is in mourning.

Sally is such a help to us both now that we are entering old age and our younger sons are a worry to us. But I feel she has not much life of her own; of course she needs to marry and, as she does not go about much, she does not meet anyone. I hope she does not grieve over her lost fiancé. She never speaks of him, but I saw her once put away a box tied up with ribbons and she blushed as she did so; I presumed it contained his letters, but I am not sure.

I have an interesting new patient, a Miss Mary Anne Provis, who unfortunately lost her wits recently. I made a point of telling Farington that she was my patient, and for once he looked out of countenance. He was one of numerous people who bought her *Venetian Secret* (how to paint like Titian, and so on) when she was a girl, for £10. Now she is 20 years older, but I wonder if the desire to trick people with this pseudo art revelation was part of an undercurrent of madness in her even then. I remember Turner always said it was nonsense, even when others were credulous. But how stupid people can be. Fancy thinking £10 would make it possible for them to paint like the Venetians!

1819

Edridge is staying in Paris with Sir George Beaumont; he is aware that he is now the object of this nobleman's benevolence, which is a strange role. Having known for so long other artists who were in trouble of one sort or another being paid for or looked after by Sir George, now he himself has come under his benevolent wing.

Of course it had been disguised on the invitation as a sketching trip, but neither man has yet done much sketching; indeed Sir George has done none. It is hot in the city and he is already getting restless. Edridge has been conscientiously attempting to draw Notre Dame from various angles, while Sir George fusses round the rooms in the Place Vendôme which they have taken. He sometimes suggests Switzerland, 'Mountains, hm?' or some other part of France.

Edridge suspects that the Baronet would prefer to go home to his beloved Coleorton, which he talks about endlessly. He has to admit Sir George is extremely kind and sympathetic but sometimes he wishes he could merely grieve for his Henry alone; even after a year the pain does not seem to recede. The church atmosphere reminds Edridge of the boy's death in Taunton and of his gravestone there; yet in some ways it is a solace to sit in the gloom of the cathedral's interior. Quite often if the organ is being practised Edridge merely sits with his head in his hands and weeps.

He is aware that Sir George, who never had any children, cannot really understand parental love. He is half amused and half touched that each night, when the Baronet reads to him, a task which he undertakes with great willingness and executes well, that he always avoids anything which might mention death.

Edridge decides one night to tell him he need not be so scrupulous as to avoid the subject, but he bluffly replies, 'My dear Edridge, I do not avoid it, I assure you.'

The next night, however, Edridge notices with some amusement that one of the poems does mention death obliquely. Perhaps, he thinks, if we are long enough together he will bring the subject in more and more until we have something like the Duke's speech on Death from *Measure for Measure*. I have heard him do that before now, at Monro's.

They often talk of their mutual friend together of an evening, while they eat. Sir George likes a good meal at the end of the day. 'But none of your French messes,' he always tells the cook. He likes good old roast beef if he can get it.

Edridge thinks Beaumont was quite relieved to hear that he might go on to Rouen and that he had written to the Doctor suggesting he join him there. 'Although you know, Edridge, he is not a man to sketch in the town. He is all ponds and bushy hills.'

'We could take our equipment out into the country too.'

'I think, however, he won't come; he is too much of a home bird,' Sir George adds, pouring them both liberal amounts of wine.

'Yes, I'm afraid you are right. He has never left Britain's shores, and why should he start now?'

'I always thought it odd,' the Baronet continues, chewing his beef noisily, 'that he sent some of his children abroad quite lately. I think Farington told me.'

154

'Yes, the two youngest, and I agree that he acts out of character. In fact I met the youngest, Alexander, in Boulogne when I was travelling to join you,' Edridge says.

'So you met him?' Sir George is quite a gossip and stops eating for a moment.

'Yes. He was sketching. Those two youngest boys seem to be following in the footsteps of his artist son, Henry; but of course he does not wish them to continue with it.'

'Quite right. Amateurs, dilettanti, that's what gentlemen should content themselves with being.'

Edridge reflects that Sir George has not actually followed his own counsel, showing sometimes at the Academy and not to very much acclaim. He wonders if he will attack Henry Monro's career in the Academy, but perhaps Sir George has realised he has no leg to stand on.

Edridge wonders whether to repeat to Beaumont his conversation with Alexander, who had been sent over to improve his French and was doing so very successfully, he said, with several pretty daughters of the family he stayed with. He had even added a wink. Edridge had not told Monro and decides not to repeat anything to Beaumont either. He can't help sympathising with the boy: at 17, of course his thoughts are full of women!

'You know Monro is thinking of retiring entirely from town, selling up?' Edridge says, pulling his chair away from the table.

'I had heard something of it, but only indirectly. Do you think it wise?' Sir George is rubbing his stomach happily.

'I think it is financial in origin; he obviously lost some of his income with that unpleasant business at Bedlam, and he still has two boys to send out in the world. I gather his wife is resisting his efforts to move, however.'

'She is an odd woman. She never liked the country, I think.'

'Oh yes, in some ways she did. She was always so aware of her squint in company and she can be quieter in the country. No company to peer at her.'

'We always want what we haven't got,' says Beaumont sagely, as though he had only just invented the idea. 'Just so long as he doesn't start selling off his collection; that would indeed be a sadness.'

'I doubt if he'll ever do that. I hear he is even planning to buy some more to put in a special room in Bushey. It has become an obsession almost.'

'What a pity it is,' Sir George leans back in his chair which creaks protestingly, 'that he has always refused to collect oils. He has a huge blind spot there, I fear. However, we must bear with each other's little ways. He is a good fellow nonetheless.'

Edridge knows that soon the conversation will move on with an awful inevitability to Turner, Sir George's pet hate, so he settles himself deeper into his chair and waits.

'He has had a rough ride lately and I suppose he must be 60. They say his protégés no longer frequent his house. In one case I should think that a hearty relief? You can guess to whom I refer?'

Edridge nods.

'Of course Monro always defends him, but what a waste of a talent. I saw some of his early work, you know, done when he was about 18 under Monro's roof. Very promising. And now look at this stuff he churns out. He's been to Scotland, you know, and was badly received there. Not surprising, of course, but he must have felt it. Apparently he has gone back to his lecturing at the Academy – perfect cheek ever to have stopped in my opinion, but he seems to have the committee eating out of his hand. Added to that he's got a new picture at the Academy, *Richmond Hill on the Prince Regent's birthday*. It's huge, and of course the usual muddle. Poorly drawn figures. He wants to court the

156

new King in waiting. He's no fool in that respect but I gather it hasn't found any favour.' Beaumont is grinning.

'I saw it, it took him two years to paint apparently,' Edridge says and yawns, hoping Sir George will take the hint and suggest going upstairs to bed.

'Two years wasted and who knows how long the mad King will continue to live. The Regent is rather premature if he thinks he will take over any day now. Did you know Turner also has a show at Fawkes's, or in fact two friends mounting shows of his work in London at present? He certainly seems to be able to find people who are taken in by his bravado with a paint brush. Did I tell you I actually bumped into him at Fawkes's show, but I turned away before he could speak? I really could not bear to have him kow-towing to me.'

Edridge wonders if that is really the way to describe what Turner would have done.

Finally he pleads a feeling of melancholy overcoming him and is allowed to escape to bed, to avoid more vituperations on the same theme.

1820

Thomas's diary

I am at last moved out of London and Hannah has got over her weeping and wailing, or at least I sincerely hope so. I am really enjoying setting up a new room for pictures in Bushey, and I have to realise that Hannah has no such fun to fill her life here. She does have Sally, luckily, but the young lads are really old enough to be leading their own lives and she mourns over the fact that she does not see her grandchildren so often now. Really she has few friends, but that is her own fault for refusing to go to dinner parties or out to the theatre all these years.

I am relieved she has Sal, but then again Sally should be finding her own life with a husband, which she has not done. I suppose I should bless the day that Sally lost her fiancé, but even though Hannah would be lonely were Sal married, I still wish the girl was not looking ever more like a spinster who has lost her chance and been left on the shelf.

It is good to hear her playing the piano to her mother, which she does much of the day, until her hands must feel really tired, but she never complains. It soothes her mother especially when she is depressed about losing her London abode.

Hannah is amazed that I have found room for all my collection and yet that I want to buy more Canalettos from Farington. I told her I would sell some of my Girtins and Cozens to make room for them, but that did not please her either, as she said with feeling that I was betraying poor Tom by selling his stuff.

I told her I am keeping one or two of his which mean a lot to me. I even offered to give her one to hang in her own boudoir. She was in a pet and so did not accept it, but I think she will eventually. She fingered it rather longingly. It is the one of Jedburgh Abbey, and I know she likes that the hustle and bustle of daily life is in the foreground as well as the abbey ruin itself.

Linnell has been negotiating the sales for me. I find he has a talent for this sort of thing, though he irritates me by talking religious nonsense half the time. Give me the established Church of England any time, not this new nonsense of Methodism and that sort of thing.

I was delighted the other day to hear that my old friend Edridge has been elected to the Academy at last. He is very pleased, despite pretending it does not matter and it has come too late. He has aged a lot since his Henry died and I wonder sometimes whether he is right and he has not much longer for this world. I pray that God will not take him yet; I have lost too many of my friends and I have few new protégés to take over from those who have long drifted away from me.

The worst thing at the moment is I worry perpetually about Alex and Jack, neither of whom will give up the idea of making a career through painting. I fear for them both but, on the other hand, I do not wish to do with them what I did to Henry. How can they both possess the talent he did? I fear neither has it, though I have to admit they do show some. I cannot keep them financially for ever, and I still feel as strongly as ever that being an artist is no real career for a gentleman.

Hannah and I no longer discuss it, because she always says it is my fault; I should never have brought young aspiring artists into the house if I didn't want my sons to follow suit. Only two out of our five sons had the sense not to dabble in paint, is how she puts it.

I retort, 'Well Sally doesn't either, that's three out of six children on your side.'

Then she gets haughty and says, 'It isn't a case of sides.'

You can see why we try to keep off the subject.

I tend to stay in my picture rooms and enjoy the peaceful company of my darlings of paint rather than of flesh, but I know this is selfish and I have to meet Sally's reproachful stare every evening when I go to dinner.

I am hardly doing any work now and feel the better for giving up all the travelling on horseback, though of course I do less sketching now I am not out and about so much. I am feeling my age. I have been troubled with toothache a lot lately and the tincture of cloves I administer hardly seems to take away the pain. I shall have to face having an extraction. My indigestion still troubles me too.

*

Linnell, father of many children, is dining with his friend Hunt, and John Varley, also a father of many, is there too.

Varley has just secured another loan from Linnell, who seems to be able to sell more pictures and remain solvent far better than poor John ever can.

Hunt is showing some of his sketch books to the other men and Varley lingers over one. 'This is very much in the style of the good Doctor,' he says. 'I don't suppose you see much of him these days, do you? I have to confess I have not been out to Bushey for ages. They say he is ageing fast, since he lost his job in Bedlam and has had to draw in his horns and give up his London house.'

'Have you seen him, Linnell?' asks Hunt.

'I certainly have, and thereby hangs a tale, which I in fact wanted to tell you both tonight. I waited until we three were alone, as it is of a rather private nature.'

160

'It all sounds very secret, even unpleasant,' Hunt says, putting away the sketchbook which seems to scorch his hands a little. He wishes he had some ale to drink but Linnell is very religious these days and he dare not produce it in front of him.

'You may know that I have been selling off some of the Doctor's collection for him, as I have some excellent contacts in that area.'

'Yes, Monro needs to sell some, they say he is buying some more Canalettos, and surely anyway he must have run out of wall space!'

'Well, this is the point, the last batch, which he calls Girtins, I know for a fact were copied by me and I think you, Hunt, also copied some at one time.'

'But surely he wouldn't pretend they are real Girtins? I can't believe he would do a thing like that.' Hunt looks upset. 'Have you got any of them with you now? I could soon tell you if it was a copy I had done.'

'No, they are not here,' Linnell says. 'You may defend him as much as you like, but I think I can admit to know my own copying.'

'But what did he say when you challenged him?' asks Hunt.

'I did not challenge him. I did not realise until I got home. I am unsure how to proceed. That is why I am talking to you now.'

'Surely,' Varley says, 'he would not dare to give them to you to sell if he knew you had done the copying. No, Linnell, I think you must be mistaken.' He says this with some reluctance, very much aware of the loan that his friend has just given him.

'You are both being very stupid. You are too influenced by the fact that he has been kind to you both, to me too when I was very young. But that doesn't mean to say that he is entirely honest. He is, as I say, trying to pass off copies

161

as originals, and I shall not hesitate to tell anyone who tries to buy them that they are not true Girtins.'

'Would it not be better to ask the Doctor, or tell him what you intend to do before you go round spreading rumours? He will be very angry.' This from Varley.

'He should have thought of that before he started to act immorally.'

Hunt is shaking his head. 'No, Linnell, he is too good a man, he is a gentleman whose very code would never allow him to do that sort of thing.'

'Well, I shall not expose him publicly as I am tempted to do; but you cannot convince me, either of you, that he is innately so perfect that he would not take a chance on making some money.' Both of his friends are staring at the table and not catching his eye. 'He behaved badly over that Bedlam business. That should have alerted both of you to his true nature.'

'How do you know? He said that it was his deputy who lived in the hospital and did not carry out his orders,' Varley replies.

'And you believe that?'

'Yes, I think so.' Varley is faltering.

'I heard that Monro never visited the hospital as regularly as he was supposed to. It's a case I'm afraid of someone who is obsessed with collecting art and does not really care who else suffers in the pursuit.'

Hunt is feeling awkward; he cannot really force his friend out of his house, but he hates to hear things about a man and his family whom he has grown to love over the years. He decides to use his infirmity as an excuse. 'I'm very much afraid, you two, that I must go and rest my leg. It really is giving me a bad time this evening. So sorry to be a bad host.'

Of course they both get up and leave with shows of sympathy, but he feels that Linnell knows it is a lie. Hunt sincerely hopes Monro will not hear of Linnell's suspicions. If only he had said he would buy the Girtins, there would have been no trouble about identifying them. However, he is not particularly rich himself. He vows to ask Linnell next time how much Monro wants for them and to see if he can raise the money. Meanwhile Linnell will surely not continue to sell paintings for Monro, and it may blow over. It occurs to Hunt that Linnell's very religiousness has not made him a kind man in every respect. He remembers now that even when new, Linnell would criticise the Doctor for trying to correct details in the pictures his fellow artists produced. 'Of all the nerve!' Linnell would say, but not in front of Monro.

1821

Thomas's diary

I feel quite numb with the pain; my friend Edridge has died, which means all my old friends are dead, as well as my son. Tom attended him and sent me word daily. Somehow or other I could not get up the energy to attend him, even though I knew that I should and I even wanted to.

Apparently his legs mortified before the end and there was little hope. Poor man, he had little happiness in the last few years, and yet he had always been such a jolly fellow before that.

And what a career! Feted once upon a time for his portraits, the latest things he did were market-day pictures with a reed pen. This gave the one I saw, at least, an interesting effect: one set in Rouen, with clear black edges to the houses. And executed when he was recovering so slowly from the death of his son, out there with Beaumont in France. What a man to paint like that when he was at his lowest ebb.

The children, especially Sal, are upset, as he was their favourite of my closest pals. I shall set up a memorial to him here in Bushey, to a great friend and consummate artist. I keep remembering how he said there were few of us left and we must see ever more of each other for that very reason, but I don't think we did in the last few years. Now I know how right he was and it is a bitter thought.

It makes me feel there cannot be long to go, and the latest blow is that Farington too has died, but at least he

164

was 74 whereas Edridge was only 52, younger than me by ten years. Farington had a heart problem, so perhaps it was not so unlikely that he would go before me, but oh, the desolation. Farington apparently fell dead outside his pew after evening service at his brother's church. Not a bad way to go after all. I suppose we shall miss getting all the art gossip now. Sir George seems really to have been affected by his death and even I miss him.

Now that the poor old King is dead, who was such a nice fellow when sane, we have a new King, my old tennis partner, now George IV. I do not hope very much for the future; he has led a dissolute life as a regent and, although the uncertainty and distress of having his father mad so often must have been hard, he did not come out of it well. He should certainly not have secretly married Mrs Fitzherbert, and then married his Queen as well.

There has been a lot of fuss about the coronation and I am very glad to be retired and quiet, contemplating my pictures out here in Bushey and not out in the grand world any more. I found Hannah loved following the scandal of Queen Caroline, how he locked her out of the ceremony at Westminster Abbey, and I promptly told her it would be better if she did not involve herself; but she really enjoyed talking to anyone she could about how terrible it was. She feels sorry for the woman because her only child died; but it is just as hard for the father and having no heir now makes it worse. Hannah told me today that the estranged Queen has died now too.

'Everyone seems to die at the moment,' was all I could say.

The man was really too old to start to become King, already 59, added to which he is so unpopular, being stoned in the street by the crowd, so they say. But then which is better, a mad king or a bad king? I wonder who will take over when he goes. I shall probably not be there to find out.

165

Turner has been in Italy, last year I believe. He must be pleased at last to be able to travel there with no difficulty. He has given his lectures this year it appears, but has not shown any picture at the Academy; perhaps he too is feeling his age, though he is as yet only 46. What would I not give to be back at that age myself with my little lads only four and three years old, instead of grown up and still a financial burden to me. The older one gets, the younger all the people below one appear. I remember when 46 would have seemed a great age.

I doubt I shall ever see Turner again, and really it is no great hardship, but sometimes I feel it would be nice to get some recognition of what I did for him and the others. Hannah lectures me, saying a bird which flies when you have rescued it as a fledgling fallen from the nest, does not turn before it goes to thank you, so why should any of your protégés? Be glad that they have at least been able to fly away. Somehow I don't find the analogy very helpful.

I miss Henry more and more. I don't see much of Tom, though he is always kind when we meet up. He is busy with the job I had and that irks me, though it shouldn't. I am glad he took it on so willingly and he never complains that he has to share it now with Tuthill. He seems to cope with the private homes perfectly well, too, and I have no worries on that score. Bob is busy too with parish affairs and his family; he is his mother's confidant more than mine. I somehow can't find it in my heart to love the two young lads and sympathise with their desire to be artists in the same way that I loved Henry. So that just leaves Sal, who is a darling but still more her mother's darling than mine.

Hannah heard me groaning as I went up the stairs the other day and asked me the reason. I passed it off as my legs hurting but really sometimes I groan at what I have made of my life in many respects.

1822

Thomas's diary

Jack has not found a job nor does he want to do anything but draw. I tried to get Reinagle's son, an artist of no mean reputation, to have Jack live there and work with him, but he demanded too much for three months' board and lodging. Jack thought me mean not to pay it, but he is now 21 and should not expect me to pay for everything. He has a terrible temper and drinks far too much.

The other day I took a step I thought I would never have to take, I locked up all my spirits and wines; I have never had to do this with my servants even and it is a shock that I have to do it with my son. He thinks his mother and Sal a soft touch, I am afraid, and sometimes gets money from them, on loan. I shall have to be more careful in my accounting when I give them money.

Hannah thinks the two lads should live together but Alex is still at Oxford. We will wait to see what he wants to do when he has graduated.

A new blow has fallen since I wrote that last piece. A severe blow. Alex has eloped to Gretna Green with someone called Henrietta Witty. I only know her name. I cut him off immediately with the proverbial shilling. Of course; why should he bring more grey hairs to his parents than they have already? He has not even finished his degree.

I stand for hours in front of my pictures, which should comfort me, but I scarcely see them; I keep thinking, why, oh why, did the first two, nay the first four, behave well, two safely married, Bob to his cousin even, and then two behave so badly. At least Jack hasn't eloped, even if he hangs around the house looking angry and trying to cadge drinks off anyone who comes to the house, to my everlasting shame.

Alex wrote to me but I tore up the letter. Sally remonstrated with me and said I should at least have read it. Hannah said nothing. She cries a lot. She did say once that she thought it was the bad blood of her sister Sarah coming out. I don't think we can really blame her, I told her dryly.

Tom is in touch with them and seems to be taking on the role of wise adviser. He wrote to the girl's father as well as to me, to say he has prevailed upon Alex and the girl to marry in London, as well as the illicit marriage in Gretna Green. At least it goes some way to making the girl respectable. Tom says he is paying for everything at present, but he implores me to forgive them. I suppose he does not want to have to go on footing their bills and rather hopes that I will do it instead. Really I shall have to pay Tom back too.

I presume I shall have to forgive them in the end. I miss seeing Alex's face around the place and Jack blames me more than ever for ignoring his brother.

We had a terrible row the other day, luckily when the women were out. He accused me of ruining both his and Alex's lives and repeated the taunts about loving my Henry more than any of my other children. When he started calling him 'Saint Henry' I finally struck him, which I much regret doing now I am calm again, but it did sober him up. He had been drinking, of course. That jibe about Henry was too much for me. But that I should strike my son. I felt like Cain! I did not tell Hannah.

Sal is anxious to meet Henrietta and have a new sister, as she calls it. She is a forgiving soul, but of course she does not have to pay for the miscreants. She tells me that the girl is pregnant. What other additions to this sorry tale can there be?

I finally wrote to Alex and suggested he try and finish his degree at least and then endeavour to get some sort of employment. I pointed out that I could not for long keep him and his family, as I am a retired man. I didn't want to sell my pictures just to keep them and I hope he would not ask me to. However, I have since decided to sell one or two of the less loved ones in my collection and send them the money; but I shall point out that I am not going to repeat the process until my walls are bare.

Jack told me that he might as well have the money now if I sold his share, rather than wait until I am dead. I was furious. What about the pleasure they give me while I am still alive? I pointed out in as cool a tone as I could muster.

Will any good come out of either of those boys? I wish we had stopped at four children after we had Sally. I suppose Hannah always hoped for more girls and they certainly would have been more biddable. Jack pointed out that I would have had to give them dowries when they married had they been girls, which annoyed me, as of course it was intended to.

*

Sally Monro is standing outside Merry Hill looking anxiously towards the road. She is feeling rather like Judas because she has gone behind her father's back for the first time in her life. A day or two earlier she and her mother had almost simultaneously agreed to try and bring the newly-weds to Merry Hill.

'Suppose we simply ask them to come,' her mother had suggested at the end of yet another long doleful conversation, and Sally had added, 'While Father is out.'

'Can we, do you think?' Hannah brightened. 'I mean, how can we find a time?'

'Let's look in his duty book as he calls it. He does have a few private calls he should make at Brooke House, I know.'

So the deed was done, Alex primed to come and Monro safely got out of the way. As she had kissed him goodbye that morning, Sally had even suggested he should linger a little to do some sketching. 'You haven't done any for ages, Father, and I'm sure it would please you on such a pretty day as this is.'

He had thanked her warmly and she had blushed with shame. However, he had complained that sitting on the ground these days tended to make him very stiff, so she is worried he will come back too soon for that reason, or that it will rain.

Alex's hired carriage is not coming, so she runs up to see that Jack knows what is happening. Yesterday he had been in such a state she had not confided in him.

She knocks on his door and a surly voice answers.

'Jack, it's Sal. I want to tell you something.' On entering she is shocked to see the state of his room, but decides to say nothing. He is lying on his bed, actually sketching the scene below his window.

'So what is it? If it's about yesterday and the money you refused to give me, don't bother to apologise.'

Sally sits down wearily.'It's about Alex and his bride, Jack. Mother and I have a little secret from Father and I hope you won't spoil things.'

He looks pleased. 'Why should I spoil things? I'm not doing him any favours. What is this guilty secret then?' And he puts down his sketch and is all attention.

'We've asked them to come here while Father is out.'

He whistles. 'So you think he won't find out, because I can assure you he will. He's nobody's fool, whatever else he is.'

'We just think if we can get them here and he finds out

170

later he will accept it. It's only his pride and Mother is so upset. I can't see another way. I don't like deception any more than you do.'

'You're wrong, I love deception! I practise it all the time. All right, I'll go along with your little game, but I warn you, I shall play the dumb innocent if Father says anything to me.'

'And do you think you could put on something clean and get the servant to shave you?'

'Yes, big sister.'

She escapes, thinking it is best not to alienate him again, by asking him please to not go about Bushey in an unkempt condition. The servants are gossiping. She sighs; really, compared with Jack, Alex's problems are minor ones.

*

Sometimes, she thinks, screwing up her handkerchief as she sits in the hall willing the bell to ring, men are too difficult, but at other times she cries in the silence of the night at the thought that she will probably be an old spinster all her life. What will happen when her parents die? She will only be a burden on one of her brothers.

She loves seeing her nephews and nieces, and Bob or Tom would doubtless take her in; the others too, perhaps, if they ever manage to get any money of their own. But it is hard to feel one's fate is decided by one man or another, and to feel love has passed her by. She had thought she was deeply in love once with her own Harry, as she had called him, but now she thinks it was probably infatuation, and she is very relieved that she had seen through him when he dropped her after her Papa was in trouble.

What strange creatures we are, she thinks, looking for the hundredth time at the clock, love seems fixed so as to blind one. When I see long-married people like Papa and

171

Mama I wonder if they ever felt it. They get on each others' nerves, but I suppose they do love each other too. Or is it just because they are accustomed to each other?

I don't ask Jack, as he would say something rude about Father. He always thinks that Papa only loves Henry so much because he is dead and therefore can't put a foot wrong. 'He did his best to stop him becoming an artist and now he mourns the fact that he would have been such a great one had he lived!' is Jack's usual argument.

Jack comes down the staircase behind her now, dressed fairly soberly, but on his way out.

'Jack, don't forget Alex and Etta are coming.'

'I shan't be long,' he says, and disappears.

She puts her hand to her brow. 'And I thought in my innocence he was going to do exactly as I asked him today.' Sometimes she gets tired of being the good one who reasons with everyone and soothes her mother with some Mozart on the piano before bedtime. She always starts fidgeting about nine o'clock and Sally knows exactly what she is going to say: 'How about a little *Eine kleine nacht musik*?'

'Mother, that means a *little* little night music,' she had remonstrated once, but her mother never really listens.

Then at last comes the sound of a carriage, and Alex is handing his wife out. Mrs Monro appears, all smiles to see them, Sally getting her share of the sweetness. Etta is shy but glad to see there are no frowns today. Jack even reappears after a while.

Alex is penitent up to a point, and speaks very highly of what Tom has done for him. No one mentions the Doctor. Mrs Monro piles food on their plates, or rather makes the servants do so, and cries. After the meal Sally spends quite a lot of time listening out for hoofbeats in case her father returns early or, if she is not doing that, looking at the sky to see if it threatens rain.

To the great relief of all, the newly-weds leave a good

172

hour before he returns. Later Sally hears her mother talking to her father after she herself has retired to bed, but only through the wall. She can hear her mother's voice but not the words, and then some fierce exclamations from him. But then it gradually settles down into a more balanced conversation, as far as she can make out, and the next morning he only gives her an odd look before saying, 'Well, Sally, it seems we have a reconciliation on our hands.' He is actually laughing.

She is very glad he didn't get to know her part in it, but reflects that he does seem happier now it has happened. Presumably they can invite Alex again quite easily. When Sally speaks to her mother she says that no one knows quite what will happen about money, but at least Monro seems to think he can manage to help them a little. No one has mentioned that Etta is to have a baby next year as yet. He will see for himself in a month or two. Mrs Monro is a changed woman, and even Jack seems to smile.

Sally is so relieved that she goes off to play a few merry tunes on the piano. Her father comes in and says how lovely it is to hear her playing like that, so she realises she must have been playing only doleful tunes. If we could sort out Jack or at least get him out of this house and doing something other than drinking, she thinks as she plays, the line between Father's brows, which has really etched itself there lately, might almost disappear.

Later that morning he invites her in to see how he has rearranged his watercolours and drawings, which he tends almost as if they were sick animals, not inanimate objects.

'Ah, you are looking at one of my early Turners. Do you know the new King has asked him to do a huge picture of the battle of Trafalgar for Saint James Palace? Two other artists are doing other victories, it seems, so he isn't the only one to be favoured. However, he is not slighted as everyone thought he would be when the old King died. He has tried so hard to curry favour and Sir George always thought he would get nowhere. He will make a good picture of Trafalgar, in my opinion. He was always good at portraying ships and the sea, though Beaumont wouldn't agree with that either,' he adds and laughs. 'He says Turner makes the sea look like whitewash and green marble!'

She is glad her father is showing her round his art rooms. Now his friends Hearne and Edridge and even Farington are dead, and most of his protégés are flown, he needs to talk about art to someone and she knows her mother isn't that interested. It would make more sense for him to talk to Jack and Alex on these topics, but he won't of course. Families are odd things, she reflects. I can't help being very fond of Father despite his rather crusty manner half the time.

She suspects he gets very depressed by the mad people he still sees occasionally, though the worst depression had been when he stopped working at Bethlem. He always blames Methodism for madness, which she thinks is too simplistic. 'All that hellfire,' he says, 'no wonder they feel anxious about what will happen when they die. The more Methodists there are, the more mad people there will be.'

She knows he talks about all this rather than about his two youngest sons, which is what really is upsetting him. And so she continues to walk round the art rooms, commenting on this and that and hoping to calm him.

1825

Thomas's diary

Terrible trouble has again befallen the family. Jack has eloped with the housemaid.

He was already a constant drain on our pockets and all our nerves were frayed wondering what drunken escapade he would be found indulging in next. But no one could have foreseen this.

All we knew of Jack's particular liking for this girl was Hannah finding them once in his room talking about his pictures. They had some of them laid out on the table near the window. He has had his own studio in London with his brother for a year or so now and he has sold some of his pictures, but I am virtually supporting them both. That a son of mine of 24 should still be supported by his father! Sally tries to look on the bright side. 'Harriet is a nice little thing,' she says, 'and has some talent of her own with a pencil and a brush.'

'Not the right kind of brush,' I said, trying to joke, though God knows I have never felt less like it. Hannah told me that when she went into his room that day the girl jumped up from the table guiltily, as well she might. She told her in no uncertain terms to get on with her work, and she curtseyed and left. Those pictures she saw on the table and thought were Jack's were perhaps Harriet's all along.

'What did I do wrong that my last two children should both elope?' I kept asking, as I lay on the sofa sipping some brandy, which Sally thought was restorative.

175

The worst of it for the Monro name is that she is a mere servant, though Henrietta, who first eloped, has proved a good wife, so perhaps Harriet may too, according to Sally who is ever optimistic.

Frederick, my nephew the soldier, has most kindly gone to try and fetch them back. Major Newton, who is a friend of his and mine, has gone too. I just hope and pray they may find them and persuade them to marry, which is probably the best thing, though that I should let such a thought into my head seems extraordinary enough.

I have had no desire to work at all and Tom has taken on the last remnant of my patients. I spend my time in the art rooms or sometimes out in the garden with the flowers that remain this autumn. When we had an early fall of snow I got the staff to put some artificial flowers into the snow; I think I must have gone a little mad myself. I saw them shake their heads a little as they did it. I had been feeling that my life was a wasteland and I had told Hannah so. The next thing I heard was Hannah telling one servant that she supposed the flowers made the snow less of a wasteland for me!

One thing I have done which I curse myself for. I managed to persuade Hannah to see a friend of mine who knows something about eyes. I think, despite herself, she thought she was well on the road to having her squint cured, after years of trying to hide it and refusing help. The sad part was that he said there was nothing to be done and this has cast her into abject misery.

She keeps saying, 'I am no good to you, Thomas, I cannot go into society and now your friends have all died and your lads have departed. If only my squint was better, I could be to you what I should always have been.'

Poor thing, I feel her own sense of desolation, though privately I think she was unlikely to have courted society, squint or no squint, after so many years without it. I try to comfort her but we are a miserable couple just now.

*

Jack is sitting reading the paper in his lodgings. 'I am now a married man!' he thinks to himself wonderingly. He tries the phrase out on his tongue, as he is alone, and it still sounds odd. However when Harriet comes back up the stairs, a little red from climbing so many steps, he throws the paper away and laughs with delight. He loves to watch her, either touchingly trying to look like a lady in her new gown, or kindly fetching some of her delicious food (her mother is a cook and she has learnt the art too). His heart always melts and he knows he has done the right thing.

He knows she feels bad about it all, though she had agreed to elope, so she had some idea what would follow. Jack knows his father is extremely upset and displeased, but hopes fervently that in the end he will be won round. He wishes he was not so afraid of him.

He hopes that Harriet is right when she says that the Doctor will be so pleased to find that Jack never touches a drop these days, that he will be glad to accept the reason for it into the family. She often sits on his knee and squeezes his cheeks, saying, 'What a lot the love of a good woman has done for you, Jackie boy!'

Jack suspects that Harriet is a better artist than he is. He is officially teaching her how to draw but he knows she has a touch that he can only envy. They both have to keep painting and trying to sell their pictures. Money is tight, though Tom has been helping them out and has assured his brother that Father will be sure to take over, when Tom has had a chance to talk to him properly about it. 'He is not going to let a son of his starve, now is he?' Tom says.

In any case it is fun to sally forth with their sketching

177

things, Harriet never seeming to tire, and if the weather is good the days are some of the best he's ever experienced. After all Jack is doing what he has always wanted to do in life, with the person he loves next to him, teasing him and saying that of course as a gentleman he must be a better painter than a jobbing artist like herself. When they are done, they start off criticising each others' efforts and end up laughing and stuffing each other's mouths with whatever they have bought for their picnic.

She cannot possibly know how glad he is to get away from that awful house in the Adelphi and the one in Bushey too. His mother forever looking miserable because of her loneliness and her squint, Sally being kind but martyred about Jack's drinking and his father hardly speaking and suspecting him of drinking some of his fine spirits. The final straw had come when Father had not allowed him the key to any cupboard in that room.

In his gloomiest moments Jack knows that he is never going to be accepted as an artist by his father. Henry was the artist; he and Alex can never aspire to be as good as him, whatever they do. And as for Mother, she had once told him that when she was expecting her last two babies she had prayed fervently that he and Alex would be girls; she had already got three boys. So disappointments all round. All the more reason for thinking only of his new life and delighting in the fact that a lovely girl like Harriet really seems to love him for what he is.

What angers Jack particularly about his father is that he lavished so much love and attention on his artist protégés. Yet despite this, he decides that his father is a snob of the worst sort.

If we do get reconciled, Father and I, it will be because Harriet wishes it, not because I do, he says to himself and he watches her tidy away the sketches and set out a simple meal on the table for the two of them.

Thomas's diary

I have had to swallow this last draught of poison, which isn't saying much perhaps, as all cups seem bitter these days. Jack has married our old housemaid, may they never live to regret it. Of course if he hadn't I would have been very upset too. Well, he is out of my hair at least. I do not know what she will do, she certainly cannot work as a housemaid any longer and he has little money. However, he does appear to be steadier by all accounts. If she can make him stop drinking I suppose we should all be grateful to her.

Hannah and Sally prevailed on me to receive them, Sally pointing out that I had ultimately received Alex and Henrietta. Though it was very odd indeed to find a housemaid now leaning on my son's arm, they seemed happy, and he certainly appeared more respectable-looking than he has done for some years. Hannah and Sally have great hopes that now he has a woman in his life he will work harder and stay sober and those awful rages will be things of the past. That is asking rather a lot of the human frame, but we can only hope.

I am most grateful to my nephew Frederick for having found them and persuaded them to marry. I felt I could not act in the matter myself, I had neither the physical nor the mental energy for the task. Sally is very grateful too, and always colours up when Frederick is mentioned, though she always says, 'Oh, don't be silly, Father,' if I say anything about there being a romance in that direction.

'He is interested in his career,' she says, 'not in women.'

'Well,' I say, 'it is good that *some* men are interested in their careers.'

'No, Father,' she says. 'There are lots of men who are. Look at Bob and Tom,' and I have to admit she is right there.

*

179

'That Harriet!' Cook says to Bob the coachman, 'she has all the luck. Fancy reappearing as Master Jack's wife.'

'Luck!' he says, 'To be married to a drunkard! Rather her than me.'

'Well, they do say that she's got him to reform. Now get out of my way; I have to get on with cooking the dinner.'

'If you believe that, you'll believe anything,' he answers and goes on trying to decipher part of the newspaper at the kitchen table.

'I'm only glad she didn't decide to come down and see us in the servants' quarters and have a good gloat, all in her fancy flounces,' she says .

'She was probably feeling awkward,' he says. 'It can't have been that easy for her either.'

'You always had a softness for a pretty face, Bob.'

The new housemaid, Agnes, who had replaced Harriet, is all agog and has watched out to see them arrive. She is the one who described Harriet's dress.

'I've heard tales they've no pennies to rub together, but I suppose she probably had a new dress to be married in at least,' Cook says.

'It doesn't look like my idea of a wedding dress,' the girl says.

The gardener comes in for his glass of small beer. 'Just seen the newly-weds,' he says, slumping down into a chair. 'I always had a soft spot for Master Jack. Reckon he had some sense to choose Harriet.'

'Even if she is a good manager they'll need more money than they're likely to get with selling those drawings they do,' Cook says, watching the gardener take one of her newly baked buns, and deftly moving the plate away from him. 'I hope Master Jack's got the sense to worm his way into his father's good books, that's all.'

1828

Thomas's diary

What a weary life mine is; all I see is death and destruction all round me. Hannah has been ailing for some months and I am just realising what a hole she would leave if she died. I have not really seen what a prop and stay she has been in all the vicissitudes of our lives together. She is pathetically grateful for what I have done for her since she has been confined to her room, which makes the tears rise to my own eyes.

Beaumont, that rock, has died, and though I haven't seen much of him lately, as he has been up at Coleorton most of his latter years, I will still feel the lack of his news and his goings on in the art world. I went to a service to honour him but felt I knew so few people there. Most have predeceased him who were his real friends.

Taken all in all I think he was a great man, though not always to my taste. He was an odd mixture of boyish nonsense, wanting to show off, and adult, mature understanding. In my opinion he was very short sighted to dismiss watercolour as of no importance, but otherwise he was a good artist himself, knew a lot about art and had good judgement most of the time. He made enemies by the score but equally he had many friends. Some say he was ever kindly and helpful, and I know myself his purse was always open to any artist he thought worthy of help. Edridge was grateful to him, though he used to tell me stories of their time in France together and laugh at Sir George's little ways.

To crown it all he has donated the best of his collection to the nation. This includes three pictures by Claude and a Rubens. I feel myself it would be nice to make the grand gesture like him, but I think my collection will have to be sold at my death; for one thing it does not rate in any one else's eyes with oil paintings, and secondly my children simply will need the money. Three of them are still more or less dependent on me.

I think I must have been too absorbed in Hannah's illness and not looking after my affairs properly. A lamp was left alight in the stables and they burnt down. We were not able to save much except the horses, which the groom heroically went to retrieve, being so guilty about leaving the lamp in the first place. Therefore I could not bring myself to dismiss him from my service, and probably he has learnt his lesson. I am obliged to borrow space in a neighbour's stables, but I have only two horses now and ride much less than I did. I kept the news from Hannah who I knew would be distressed. For myself I was only too relieved it was not my pictures that burnt.

I have actually tried this year once again to bring on a young protégé as in the past, but singularly failed. Welby Sherman, whom I had heard good things of, came to stay and rode out for the day to sketch with me.

I was rather dubious as I did not really think much of what he showed me of his work before we left, and, though he certainly worked hard and it was a lovely day for it, I was very disappointed at the results he showed me that evening. I felt I could hardly hold out any hopes for him by asking him to stay on further and I was also set about with worries and cares. So I probably was a little curt when I offered him the carriage the next day to take him home, but he accepted it almost with alacrity, so I presume he too was not happy with the fruit of his labours. He also probably did not find me an engaging companion, a shadow as I am of my former self! It has left an unpleasant taste in my mouth, however, when I recall the fun I had once with Varley and the others. I remember that time when Cotman got into the field with a bull and how Varley told him to first climb up a tree and then crawl through the hedge! How we laughed when he scrambled up that tree and wouldn't come down for ages.

I'm afraid Varley has had to compromise in many ways as his family grew. He now has two more children by his second wife but at least she is a better spouse than the last, by all accounts. Varley is mixing gum and varnish with his water colours now to make them look more like oils! And it was only back a few years, 1816 I think, that Varley was setting out his ideas on watercolour in his *Treatise on the Principles of Landscape Design*. I never heard that it did very well as a piece of reading matter, but I am glad he did it, anyway.

I must not forget I am an old man now, nearly 70, though looking at the sketches I made that day with Varley and Cotman I flatter myself that my talent has grown rather than diminished with my age.

The latest blow to my children is that Alex's wife, over whom there was so much trouble, has died in childbirth, along with the baby. She has given him three babies in three years but only little Donald is alive today. I never grew fond of her, indeed we did not see them overly much, but since her death I have grown fond of the poor little orphan boy and Alex himself is at his wits' end.

Hannah has kindly suggested that he and the boy come and live with us for a time. I do not see it as a long-term solution, but it may be the only thing as far as Alex's finances are concerned. I think that Sal also feels I need my poor old crabbed heart warming with a child, which may well be true. But my children and grandchildren are still my pictures, as far as solace goes. I spend much of my time nowadays in my dressing gown, merely pottering among the pictures. Sally comes and tuts over me and tells me I must get dressed in case anyone visits, but sometimes I really cannot be bothered. They will have to take me as they find me, I tell her.

I see Jack and his Harriet from time to time. She is a giggly little thing but Jack does seem very fond as a husband, and I must admit her own art work is not bad. As for Jack's I prefer his style to Alex's though I would not admit it to anyone. Alex looks as if he has ruled all his verticals and horizontals with a ruler. It is a very strange phenomenon, though I have not dared criticise him.

Tom tells me what goes on at Bethlem with Wright and Tuthill, who seem to war with each other continually. When he tells me these stories I stop wishing I was back in harness and am heartily glad I am out of it all. The Governors are of course as penny-pinching as ever. I suppose Tom does not mind as he still has the elasticity of mind which goes with youth, or comparative youth.

As for Bob, his wife is a bit of an invalid and they have no children. He too visits more especially now his mother is ailing. From hints he has dropped I think he blames me for not being a warmer husband, as he sees it; but no one can really tell what a relationship is like except those in it.

I find it a very bitter thing to be criticised even mutely by one of my own offspring over my marriage. Hannah and I are close in many ways.

*

John Linnell is laughing over a letter sent to him by his son-in-law Samuel Palmer, a man not much younger than himself. It is about Welby Sherman, whom both artists know quite well, on the occasion of his going to sketch with, or rather for, Monro. Palmer has no time for anyone of that ilk and in his letter he does not spare the Doctor. Linnell

184

has mixed feelings about Monro too, and is not much surprised that things did not turn out too well for poor Welby.

'In a brick field?' he says to himself, looking up from the page. That doesn't sound much like Monro! He usually likes sketching ponds and trees. Of course Palmer had a 'field' day with that one! He laughs again but also winces, when Palmer calls Monro's protégés 'sky sloppers and bush blotters'. He certainly does not mince his words. But then Palmer has not had much success as an artist himself; maybe part of his vehemence stems from jealousy of the more successful of those protégés, in whose number Linnell may count himself.

Linnell has been very vigilant since the time he caught the Doctor cheating, watching to see if he ever tried selling any other pictures made by his trainees as originals. 'If he had done,' Linnell had told Palmer, 'I would have been down on him like a ton of bricks.' But Linnell also sometimes remembers Monro more warmly; after all he had taken him up quite young and helped him. 'Always learn from nature!' Monro had said. It had been the best advice ever.

Finally he puts the letter away in his pocket and stands rather soberly looking down at his latest painting. Had he himself ever blotted a bush or slopped in a sky?

Thomas's diary

The event I dreaded and foresaw only too clearly happened last week. My darling Hannah died, leaving me so lonely. Thank God I have Sal still with me, though I know to think so is selfish, and Alex and the boy. When Hannah was sinking I was able to whisper my regrets to her, that I had not really taken her into my confidence as much as I should

185

and so on, and she pressed my hand and cried and I cried too, and still do cry. She was ever affectionate to me and I blame myself for not always being able to see through the fuss and the complaints about her squint disenabling her from going out anywhere, to see the true unselfish person she was. Before she ceased speaking she told me she was sure we would meet again in Heaven, and I was too cowardly to gainsay her, though I am less certain that we shall recognise each other above the clouds. I nodded and smiled and she was happy, I think.

Sally and Alex are wonderful to me, but they are not of my generation and have their own affairs and lives to lead. I heartily wish I could have gone first, but then she would have been alone, so that is a selfish thought.

There is a huge blank in my life, that is all I can say.

I hear that Turner, too, has been stricken by the death of his nearest and dearest, in this case the old father, who I suppose was almost a wife to him in many ways, though that sounds peculiar. They say he is with Lord Egremont at Petworth a good deal these days, partly as he cannot bear to be in the empty house without his father. He originally called it Solus Lodge and he is now very Solus.

They say he is looking shabby and eccentric and his lectures at the Academy are totally intelligible and mumbling, worse than ever. He is almost as much of a wreck as I am, but at least I do not show any shabbiness or mumbling behaviour to the world.

However, he has been to Rome, so he does not cease to travel nor to work. Quite a good story emerges from that which I wish Farington was still here to relish: apparently Turner did a *Forum Romanum* for Soane's museum in Lincoln's Inn, a huge thing; and Soane returned it! I'm not sure of the reason but Turner would not be too pleased with that. I would love to know what financial agreement they came to, for I can't believe Turner was presenting it to the museum for nothing! I have to take my hat off to him for continuing to travel and work so hard all the same, but then he *is* 16 years younger than me. At 54 I was in my prime, though I *was* ill that year, but it was before Henry died, before my disgrace. Yes, I can say I was in my prime then. When I see little Don, as we call him, running about on the lawns so carefree, I shudder to think what may be in store for him; but thank God we do not know what will happen after we have reached 55 or so in our lives, when we begin them with such hope and optimism.

1830

Sally is in her parlour, engaged in writing a letter to her father. She is a married woman now, at the age of 36, a time when almost everyone had given up hoping she would find someone to love. The Doctor has been delighted for her and pooh-poohed her worries that he would now be too much alone. She was grateful for that, especially when she knew how much he missed Hannah. Thankfully he is fond of Frederick, her cousin and now her husband. And he still has Alex and Don most of the time, though Alex is courting a rich woman in the neighbourhood, which is all to the good as far as he goes. One less child for her father to help with money. And to be fair, Jack is doing better; he and Harriet manage most of the time.

'Frederick and I are replanning our drawing room,' she writes, 'to make my new piano the centrepiece of the room. We are deep in choosing a new wallpaper, but we always bear in mind that we must do justice to our new picture you gave us for our wedding present. We are keeping the pattern discreet, so it does not clash with the blues and mauves of the picture.'

She stops writing for a moment, aware that her father will be more interested in his present than in the decor of her room. 'We are so grateful that you gave us one of your favourites! You cannot imagine how many times a day we both stop and gaze at it.'

She fiddles with her pen and wonders whether to say

what is on her mind, that her father should think of moving out of Merry Hill to somewhere smaller, once Alex leaves. If, that is, he does. She knows the difficulty will be the picture collection which her father will not countenance leaving behind, even in part. Perhaps if she softens him up by talking of his own art and how she hopes he still goes about sketching whenever he feels well enough, then she can come onto the more vexed topic gradually.

'Frederick was asking me just yesterday if you had been out at all at your sketching now the weather is improved. I very much hope this is the case. He also wondered if you ever see any of your protégés nowadays. I'm sure you follow their careers with just as much interest as you ever did.' She waits for the words to come which will express her concern for his keeping up so big a house if Alex moves, but nothing seems to fit, so she moves on.

'What did you think of our "new" King dying? I remember you telling us that you had once played tennis with him as a young man. I hope the new Sailor King, as they call him, will prove a good ruler.' She does not add what she is thinking that this brother does not seem to have a much better history as a family man than George IV did. Fancy leaving your partner of so many years with all those children, even if she were an actress. Did that make it any less painful for the woman? Here she knew both her husband and her father would disagree, so she sighs and tries to hunt for better topics.

'It seems extraordinary to think that just a few months ago I had no idea that I would be sitting here married to my dear Frederick. You seemed to hint that I had been keeping my feelings quiet for a long time before he proposed, but in fact I was at first only grateful to him when he helped out with getting Jack married to Harriet. He says he fell in love with my piano playing before he fell in love with me; so I should be grateful to you for making me practise! Tonight he has asked me to play some Bach partitas.'

Here Sally breaks off and studies her fingers which are slightly misshapen. She sighs again. 'We are looking forward to coming to see you as soon as we can. Your ever loving daughter, Sally.' She finishes off with a rush and gratefully blots and seals it.

*

Alex, his new wife Lucy, and old Monro are spending a few days nostalgically revisiting the places Thomas knew so well round Fetcham. In his own happiness Alex has included his father, and at last the two would-be artists are enjoying sketching together, whenever the Doctor's health allows him to descend from the carriage and take up his pencil again.

They have even been back in the old house, by kind permission of the present owners, and the Doctor has proudly shown his son some of the improvements which he made there and which have not been altered since. Alex had been only three when they left the house and therefore cannot remember anything about it.

They are now sitting with their backs against a tree trunk and with Lucy a few yards away doing some sewing. Both men are drawing the valley which lies in front of them, and the mossy-roofed farm house to their left. The Doctor tries not to look too often at Alex's drawing, for he finds his son's delight in ruled lines most daunting.

Finally he puts his notebook down and leans more heavily against the tree. 'I've been meaning to tell you, my boy, that I intend to move out of Merry Hill. I have bought a plot of land not far away and am using a modified form of the Fetcham house as a plan for my retirement home.' He laughs to show that he does not care too much about the reasons for the move.

'Well, Father, it seems an excellent plan. I know Sal has recently been worried that you have too much to do in running Merry Hill.'

He does not mention the art collection, hoping his father will elucidate.

'I have seen to it that I shall be able to house the collection,' he continues, 'although I expect you know I plan to sell it on my death. I think the money will be useful to you all.' There is a pause while a wasp comes to hover about Lucy and Alex goes to shoo it off.

'It occurred to me you two might like to take over Merry Hill from me. Seems a shame for it to go out of the family. Well, you must think it over between you. I hope that there will be other children as well as Don, one day, to fill the rooms.' Lucy blushes.

Alex promises his father to think it over. Indeed he is congratulating himself on not having had a tense moment with the old chap since they came away; but perhaps this is premature, because on the way home Thomas comments on someone they see riding along the road. 'He's the type now who will have the vote in the next election. You see how the country goes to the dogs.'

'Well, Father,' Alex begins, wondering what is wrong with the man they have just passed. 'Things must change. It is no good us clinging on to rotten boroughs with maybe one person or two to vote for an MP, while the new places like Manchester hardly have anyone to represent them.' He stops because he notices his father's face is drawn with pain. His legs are hurting him, no doubt.

'Society is like milk, it never improves by being shaken up. Look what happened to France!' Thomas manages between jolts of the carriage. After a few minutes he starts again, 'I suppose you like these new railways do you? With your newfangled ideas. Man wasn't meant to travel fast, in my opinion.'

191

'Well, Father,' Alex starts again. 'I think there will be advantages . . .'

'And disadvantages: the countryside all swallowed up, dirt, noise . . .' but he takes his son's hand. 'Take no notice of me. I'm just as bad as my father was before me. He hated change as he got older. Now I'm old and I am repeating in spirit the things he said to me, and of course you are saying the same sort of things I said to him.' He laughed wheezily. 'I'm really only taking my mind off the jolting of the carriage. I shall be glad when we get back to the inn.'

1833

Will Turner is sitting looking out to sea, having his hair cut. Sophie Booth is the woman cutting it.

'Do you want a widow's peak?' she asks laughing.

'Only if you're the widow!' He thinks of his last widow, Sarah Danby, someone he sees no longer, though they were happy enough for a while. This one is a lot older than Sarah would be now. She has only recently been widowed, however, just as Sarah was when Will ... well, in fact, he had had her before her husband died.

John, Sophie's husband, has died this year; a man much older than herself, so she had always known she would be widowed young and they had often joked about it earlier on, or so she told Will. She is comfortably off now; partly because their son died, so she had the money which would have gone to him. Her son Dan by a former marriage still hangs about the place at times. But she lives alone now much of the time, though in the summer other lodgers occasionally come.

She lives in a cottage very near the sea in Margate, with an inn on one side and a custom house on the other. There is plenty of life to observe from the front windows and Will always lodges in the front, where the waves on stormy days seem almost to pound in upon him. This is where they are now in fact.

Booth was a nice enough chap, although at first when Will turned up in Margate and asked for a room he was a

193

little suspicious of him. 'An artist, you say?' He had peered at Will in the darkness of their little hallway. 'And how often would you be wanting the room?'

At the sight of money, however, his tone had changed and he was happy to let Will stay in the same room at fairly short notice. 'I didn't know artists earned good money,' he had said once.

Sophie is less intelligent than Sarah, though perhaps that isn't saying a lot, but she makes up for that lack by being very kindly, easy company and a good cook. She is quite interested in Will's painting but she will take a hint if he growls that he wants to be left alone, and she doesn't pass judgement on what he paints. Her husband had used to suggest possible pictures, such as the crowd of people getting on and off the steam packet, but Will had managed to silence him by saying he was more interested in nature than people.

'You do the sea very accurately,' Booth used to say, 'but some of what you paint seems to me like a blur.'

Will had laughed to himself, thinking that he and old Beaumont would have a lot in common! All except for the sea, which Beaumont hadn't been very flattering about. 'Green marble and soapsuds', Beaumont certainly had a good turn of phrase!

Although Margate is a fashionable resort, Will doesn't think the Booths have ever moved in any circle except a local one and they have never realised he is famous.

She had had a little weep over Will when he had come to Margate after her husband's death. 'I was very lucky in both my husbands,' she said, 'though my first did leave me penniless at twenty-six. Mr Booth, although retired when I met him, was a great help to me, both with himself and his money, though I say it as shouldn't,' and she laughed a little uncertainly. 'Of course this little venture of our lodging house has helped.'

194

This summer Will has come more than usual; the weather has so far been fine for sea journeys and Will is enjoying being a comforter to this woman. He is delighted that his seascapes are improving by the minute and it is good to get off the steam packet and be sure of a hearty hot meal in that little kitchen.

Turner has to admit he misses his old Dad very much, and being with Sophie he is able to mingle his grief with hers when she talks of her old husband and how she misses him. Once she told Will she missed his hugs particularly.

Then one day quite recently, things had begun to change. She had put two mackerel down on the table to cook for their meal later, as she and Turner were the only ones in the house. Will had remarked on their colouring and took out a pencil and began to sketch.

It was almost funny, he thought afterwards; she had taken much more notice of this picture than any he had done from her front window, although she pretended to be blunt with him, telling him he was in her way and threatening to cook them before he had finished. Finally when Will had finished he told her she could have the picture if she liked and she was very pleased and put it on the wall, nailing it at the top without a frame.

'Now,' she said, 'we'll eat them,' and they proceeded to do so. While they chewed she kept looking up a the picture and after a while she said, 'That one's winking at me! I swear I saw it.'

'Too much beer!' he had said, laughing.

When they had eaten she had said, 'I've stuffed myself, I feel like a lie down now,' and she sat down firmly on the sofa and swung her legs up. She is already getting quite fat in the hips, though younger than me, he thought.

Well, Turner did not know quite how it was but soon he was sitting on what space was left on that sofa beside her and even later they were upstairs in her bedroom.

'Shall I call myself Mr Booth?' he had whispered to her. 'The third Mr Booth!'

'My first was Pound,' she said, 'Henry Pound.'

'And did he get his pound of flesh?' and Will had pinched her.

She hadn't understood him but she laughed a lot. He found her jolly and easy and luckily past the age when likely to have children. He had enough already with Sarah's two.

'I shall call myself Admiral Booth,' he said. 'It has a certain ring to it. What do you think? I have done enough sea pictures to qualify me for the title after all.'

She had merely ruffled his hair. Then she said, 'I don't think John would mind seeing us together like this. He always liked you. And you've got plenty of money you say! That helps too.'

'More money than youth,' Will had said.

'Oh, I'm used to old men,' she had answered, and giggled.

Thomas's diary

I am now 74 and a tired old man. My two friends Farington and Beaumont died at this age, and although I know we cannot dictate the time of our death, I am ready and almost eager to go. I moved into my new house and I should have thought that would give me pleasure, but, although it is everything I wanted, I still feel little interest in it. The family has moved on or passed on to another life. I hope and trust that the afterlife will include much beauty and even many pictures, so that I will not miss my collection too much.

As for my protégés, they haunt my dreams, but that is probably because Varley made the journey to see me recently. I was very glad to hear his news. Life is hard for him but he is ever jovial and seems mostly to make ends meet. He would not hear of my giving him any money. Linnell is putting figures into his landscapes for him now they are obligatory following this new fashion for illustrating Scott's novels; but he expects to be paid for it. When I looked annoyed, Varley was quick to defend him. 'He has been most kind to me in many emergencies and he has a family of his own to support. I suppose you could say he has been lucky that what he paints is more popular with the public than what I produce, but I do not envy him his talents nor his money.'

Varley had news of Cotman, though he does not see him. He says that although Cotman suffers from bouts of melancholia, he is teaching the daughters of a local Norfolk bigwig, but also doing a lot of topographical work to form a book of Normandy castles and ancient buildings. Varley shook his head and said that Cotman is using much indigo in his landscapes and experimenting with a sort of flour glue to thicken his pigments. 'He is trying one thing after another, it seems,' he said. We were both of the opinion that Cotman lost his way after doing so well up in Yorkshire. His inability to be elected to the Water Colour Society, the successor to his and Girtin's Brothers, was a sad blow.

'I can only think it was due to his personality and not his art,' Varley said, and I agree. He should never have left London. It was as though, like a child who does not get on with his fellows, he decided he didn't want to play any more and sulked. Poor Cotman: he too has children who wish to be artists it seems. I hope they will succeed better than him.

Alex came yesterday and found me as usual in my dressing gown and among my collection. I showed him for the first time my own sketches in a portfolio and he was very interested. I suppose he had seen me before with them, but never really showed much desire to look properly. He took one out and went into the bigger room where my

Girtins hang. He came back quite excited and asked if I had ever noticed how like Girtin's details of distant trees were to mine. 'Which came first, his or yours?' he asked. 'I suspect it was you influencing him.'

I was absurdly pleased. But it was only after that he asked specifically for a De Wint picture of Lincoln Cathedral and the river at sunset. He knows I will sell the collection but suggested the price of this could be deducted from whatever money came to his share. He said he and Lucy both adored this particular scene. It set me thinking that I might ask all my children to choose one, and the value could be deducted from their inheritance.

I only wondered afterwards if Alex had said that about Girtin to soften me up so that I would agree about the picture . . . I am getting a suspicious old misery!

I have not yet mentioned Turner. Of course I don't need Varley to give me news of him. He is always in the public eye or, rather, mouth. Varley was agog with the news that JMW has a new woman in his life, but not a soul mate, some lodginghouse keeper in Margate it appears.

We discussed his style, which has changed. He is no longer comprehensible or liked by the public, though he is still a public figure and commands good prices. I detect in his latest stuff a longing to return to watercolour, but his colours are often too bright and his outlines too blurred for my taste. Hearne never liked him even in the old style and sometimes I agree, though I do boast still that I have influenced JMW, and I keep close to me his album of early paintings. I think on balance that his name will live. I often sit and ponder about how mine will not and this I mind, but life isn't fair and he has some genius which I allow I never possessed. He is single-minded in a way that I never could be or was; he didn't have children, or rather, when he did, he did not allow them in as family. His beloved father worked for him and adored him, which is what he wanted.

Sex he got when he wanted it. Perhaps that is the way to live, certainly if you are egocentric like him. I can never forget what he did to his mother, or forgive it. I suppose the father and the son took sides against her; if that sister of his had lived, the woman might have fared better.

It must matter in the eyes of God, surely. I often ponder the question nowadays: how our Maker will rate genius against immorality.

And now to my dreams! A few nights after Alex had asked about the De Wint, I ate a large supper, rather at the urgings of my faithful butler than anything else, and I dreamt very vividly. Perhaps the cheese I ate at eleven was the cause.

In my dream Sir George, Farington and Hearne were all gathered in my painting room. Hearne had the picture by De Wint that Alex asked for, in his hand, and I came forward to remonstrate with him for removing it from the wall.

'But it has to do battle with Turner's latest picture,' Hearne said, holding it up as another picture advanced towards it. It wasn't Turner's latest at all, it was *Hannibal crossing the Alps*, in all its hugeness, which now came across, lifted as it were by invisible hands, and started to beat against the De Wint.

'Ha,' I said, 'this is exactly like *The battle of the pictures* that my father showed me of Hogarth's when it was engraved.'

Beaumont started cheering on the Turner, which of course, in the rational light of day, I realised he would never have done, and Hearne and Farington were cheering on the De Wint watercolour. I think I merely stood there keeping an eye on my other pictures in case they too flew off the walls. In the end, of course, the bigger picture won and the poor De Wint lay torn and dishevelled on the floor of my octagonal room.

So vivid was the dream, that on waking I immediately went to the room in some distress, to find of course that the picture was hanging there exactly as I had left it.

I returned to bed, taking a little brandy with me, as by now I was thoroughly awake, my mind racing. I kept wondering what had caused me to dream so vividly of that Turner, which I had not thought of these 20 years. Of course the De Wint was on my mind, but why should my old friends have so vividly been recreated in my mind, and what is more, that picture of Hogarth's which my father had shown me? I had never liked it, but he admired the man and wanted me to benefit from his knowledge of the art world. Perhaps I dreamt that in memory of him. After all, my father sold his collection to start us children off in the world.

I couldn't help smiling grimly to myself at the outcome of the battle of the pictures in my dream. Of course the big guns of oil painting won over the grapeshot of a watercolour. I thought that I should re-dream it the other way round. Why did I dream it like that? I had betrayed my own convictions.

A day or two later I dreamt again. In the meantime I was trying to work out if there was any message relayed through the first dream, though usually I would have pooh-poohed such an idea as nonsense. However it didn't seem to me to tell me that I *should* give it to Alex, nor help me to decide whether Jack and Alex as artists themselves, should inherit pictures while the other three should not, which had been my thought just before composing myself to sleep. After all, the others are not particularly interested in art in any form. But then if I only gave those two boys pictures I would much rather give Alex the De Wint which he wanted than give anything to Jack, who has been nothing but a trial to me for most of his life.

I dreamt that our old dog Mallord, who was of course

called after Will Turner, started barking and would not stop. Perhaps one of our existing dogs did bark, though the servants heard nothing. I asked them this morning. Mallord, of course, is long dead. At all events I heard the barking very clearly and the next thing was that Turner himself appeared in the room. But he looked as he was at 17, not as he is now at 58. I turned on him.

'Why did you not wait to be announced?' I asked. 'You are abominably rude! Mrs Monro will be incensed.'

'The door was not locked,' he said, 'and the dog's barking has announced me in any event.'

'I suppose you know that he is your namesake,' I said.

Instead of replying he asked, 'Where is Tom Girtin? I'm looking for him.'

'Girtin is dead,' I said.

'Have you got his *White House*?' he asked, seizing me by my cravat and practically throttling me.

I managed to get myself free. 'I wish I had,' I said. 'It is one of his greatest works.'

'My mother wants it,' he said.

'Your mother? But she's . . .'

I was going to say 'dead,' but he interrupted me. 'I know, she is in Bedlam but the committee tell her she may have it on her wall. You could at least let her have that to comfort her; you have not done much else to help the poor inmates.'

I was so incensed that this time I grabbed him by the throat. 'You poor specimen of humanity! You are the one who should have helped your mother, not me!'

'No, Thomas Monro, it is *you* who are to blame,' he bellowed. And at that I woke up, sweating in terror.

Despite getting up to relieve myself and then proceeding downstairs to get a drink, I could not get back to sleep and lay awake with Turner's word ringing in my ears. *Was* I to blame? After all I had got her into Bethlem for him and his father, and all because I did not want to lose him as a . . .

201

well, not as a friend as he was never that, but as a protégé or acquaintance. Then common sense prevailed and I blamed them for putting her away, but of course I had expedited it for them. How would I plead before my Maker? Guilty? I was afraid so.

The third night I dreamt again and of course I dreamt of Henry. But this man was at the same time my son and yet not like him in appearance. How then did I know it was him?

In his hand he held one of my pictures by Cozens, while Jack, his brother, held up a Canaletto.

Jack said, 'I shall take this when Father dies and no one will be any the wiser. He owes it me in any case for always preferring you to me.'

Henry was mute but Sally came into the room with the Turner album. 'And this is to be mine for caring so long for Mother and Father with no help from the rest of you,' she said and sat down to start turning the pages.

Henry spoke up. 'Take it, Turner's rubbish anyway. Hearne told me so when I was fifteen.'

At that Alex's dead wife entered, dressed as a shepherd-ess. She carried Gainsborough's camera lucida which I still have as a memorial to that genius. 'And I will have this because no one wanted me in the family and so I am owed it.'

At this the whole Select Committee who brought about my downfall came running in to the picture room and proceeded to unhook a picture each and run off with it. 'He shall have nothing. He neglected the mad folks and must be punished!' they called out, as they ran across the garden.

The next thing, Varley and Cotman appeared, shaking their fists at me. 'He only wanted to get his hands on our work,' they said. 'He never cared for our real merit. He never wanted to help us.'

I peered round in what now seemed to be darkness and saw that Hunt now appeared to be sitting in the corner in that old carriage he used to be pulled about in. The shafts were not connected to the horse but lying on the floor, so that he was tipped up slightly in it. And I could see his lame leg.

'Help me,' I called. 'I was kind to you. You have to admit that, Hunt!'

But I awoke before Hunt could do or say anything.

I was so upset by this dream that, though I do not usually like to awake the servants in the night, I rang the bell over and over and at last one of them came, yawning and half dressed. He was all concern for me, because he saw how I sweated. It was good to have some candlelight and I lay awake some time with some negus and a book to soothe me. He insisted on rekindling the fire, to give me some cheer, he said, and watching the shadows of the flames on the walls did give me some relief.

Sally came the next day and I told her about the dreams, though not every detail. I told her too that Alex had asked for the De Wint. I asked her what I should do about the others, including her, did they each want a picture in the same way?

I was afraid the continued indecision was making me dream horrible things, and she suggested I do what I had first thought, offer each of them a picture and deduct the value of it from their legacies. She then went in and chose her picture, one of Girtin's, though of course not the *White House*, which is not mine. I was glad she chose Girtin as I love his work very much. I think perhaps she was thinking of her mother's taste, too, in this.

Jack came and chose a Turner sketch. He is sensible, it will probably accrue in value. I half expected he would choose a Canaletto as he had in the dream! Only Bob and

Tom were left now, but they chose to keep their legacies entire. They already have a picture each that I did, and one by Henry. They say that is all they want.

After this I thought the dreams would be a thing of the past, especially as for several nights I had been free of them. But I had one more dream.

This time it was Hannah who came to me, with her sister and the late King George III. They were arm in arm and kissing. The King said, 'You played tennis with my son and that's why you limp. Serve you right. He is a monster.'

Hannah said nothing but her sister said, 'Georgie's my darling. He loves me. You can't stop that however much you say he's mad and hide in his room and spy on him.'

I looked at Hannah, hoping she would help me, and suddenly I realised that her squint had gone and that now she was the most desirable woman in the world. I reached out for her but she merely said, 'Go and kiss one of your pictures; you always loved them best. I won't let you kiss me till you have kissed each one of them.'

'Hannah, no!' I screamed and woke once more, but this time half out of my bed.

Sally got the doctor the next time she came to see me, and he took some blood. I didn't want him to but he insisted. After that I had no more dreams, but I felt very weak indeed.

I often lie and think about these dreams and how much of my life had come into them. I was glad that I had not really dreamt of Bethlem itself nor of any of my madhouses or patients. Dreaming of my artistic life had been bad enough. And of my family.

*

Sally Monro is calling on her father, and is unsurprised but still exasperated to find him in his dressing gown at three in

204

the afternoon, as usual doing the rounds of his picture gallery.

'Father,' she says in a voice that he knows means business. 'Frederick and I think that the time has come for you to move in with us. No,' she holds up her hand to silence him, 'I know what you are going to say, that you have only just moved in here and so on, but these dreams you have been having worry me and you can't deny you are finding things more difficult physically. Why don't you change your mind and come. We would make you very welcome.'

'Thank you, my dear,' Thomas is trying to find a polite way of saying that he will certainly not leave his pictures behind and has no intention of moving.

'But,' she fills in for him, 'my pictures!'

'Exactly so. I fear you will have to bear with me staying on here. I know it means visiting me, but at least you will be spared all the bother of helping me move again and of caring for me in your own home.'

'It isn't a case of bother, you know that, Father,' and she takes his hand.

'If only Hannah was here still,' he says, partly to fill up the gap and partly hoping she will not harp on about his moving. He is not prepared for her next remark.

'Well, Father, I hope if she did come back, you would treat her a bit better than you did.'

He stares in amazement. What has happened to the pliant creature who always did what he told her?

'Sally!' is all he can say, and to his horror tears appear in his eyes.

'Sorry, Father. I know you feel things more these days. But both Bob and I often talk of how little time you spent with her; it was always your protégés or your patients or your pictures.'

'But I . . . well she . . . she never wanted to come out with

205

me because of her squint and she hated meeting the protégés so . . .'

'Now don't go on so, Father,' she says, getting up to go.
But he is left with the urge to try and argue away the guilt
that the last dream and their conversation had engendered.
After all, Hannah was the one who refused to go out; and
she had the children, which was her happiness, and so on.
Finally to comfort himself he says aloud, 'Of course I could
not have got where I did without her help. Thank you,
Hannah.'

Thomas's diary

My leg throbs painfully these days when I get into my
carriage to go to church, and I need someone to help me
out of it and into the building. It is about my only outing
these days, but it is wonderful to see the delights of nature
as the spring advances. Sometimes as I go into the old
building I am filled with a conviction that I am leaving God
behind me in the trees and sky and not meeting him inside
the dark interior. I still itch to get my pencil in my hand to
record even these views I know so well. I have more
headaches than I used to and there is something very wrong
with my digestion as well. I seem some days to be one big
ache and then I do not even venture as far as church.

I have been spending much of the days in bed with very
short excursions to my gallery lately. I shall probably not
see the summer out. I long to lie in the grass again hearing
the skylark singing above my head and the clouds racing
across the blue. The worst of dying is being in the dark.

I amused myself the other day when I was bed-bound,
but with my pillows heaped up so I could see out of my
window into the trees, by trying to write my own obituary.

I worry that my work with the mad will be overshadowed by my dismissal from Bethlem; better therefore to dwell at some length on what I have done for the careers of various well-known artists.

It amused me for some time, and then both my hand and my mind grew weary. Would anyone really think I had done much for Turner? Ungrateful cub, he would probably say nothing about me at all if asked. Girtin? Who cares for him these days? Yet these two were probably the greatest geniuses and those who came after nothing in comparison.

All the same, I have had a singular life. I must leave posterity to decide if I rated at all in the great scheme of things.

*

It is June 1833 and there is a huge crowd at Christie's for the fifth and last day of the sale of the late Dr Monro's pictures.

A small untidy figure can be seen making several purchases, mainly of Thomas Girtin's pictures, though he is also bargaining for the odd Dayes and de Loutherberg.

On his way out he is accosted by Dr Burney, famous musician of the day.

'Turner! How are you? I haven't seen you for . . . well, it must be many years. You are quite a recluse I think these days.'

'Busy, Dr Burney, always busy!'

'I see you are busy, buying up some of the sketches by your old associate Tom Girtin.'

'Yes, I always admired his work, even when we were 17 and copying at the old doctor's. I notice you have the bad taste to admire those things I did then,' and he pointed to the heap near Burney's hand which he had bought. 'They mean nothing to me now.'

'But I admire everything you do, Mr Turner,' Burney replied graciously, and with some trepidation at Turner's rather savage air.

'Oh well, perhaps they are not so bad, considering they were got by the good doctor for half a crown and a bowl of oysters.'

Burney turned with a bow, and meeting an acquaintance further on in the crowded room, told him of the encounter. 'I think old Turner was quite flattered by what I said. He actually smiled and became a little less saturnine for a minute. But I could not help noticing that he did not buy any of his former patron's work.'

'Gratitude is not one of Turner's strong suits,' his companion replied. 'All the same someone has bought them and Monro has made a mint of money, or at least his children have. Let's hope they deserve it.'